*To
Sheri*

Someone's Story

His Web site is By B.A. Bellec

Sheila, thank you for the push and help. You knew this weirdo didn't belong where he was.

Jessica, your love and support changed me into a better person.

Mom, among many things, you taught me how to learn, which is invaluable and everlasting.

Michaela and Peter, thank you for the years of friendship when I wasn't my best self.

Bruce and Dad, I felt like I had to put distance between me and my past to grow, but I lost you guys along the way.

To the people who saw this before I published, your feedback was so important. Thank you for being a part of the process.

Everyone else...sorry. This is an apology for not being present. This was me learning. It hurt to write this, but I am so glad I felt all your pain.

Foreword

THIS one day I decided to befriend a smart, capable, loner weirdo that I worked with. It turned out to be one of the best decisions I've ever made. Even though he had a lot of barriers, I managed to get closer than anybody had in a very long time. A few months later, he handed me an envelope with a USB stick and a letter. The letter was such a compelling statement of friendship and trust that it brought me to tears. On the USB stick was a novel that he had written, and the letter mentioned how I was the first person outside of his immediate family to read this novel. I was super surprised and so grateful for the level of trust. I'll be honest, I was a little scared too – what if it wasn't good? I am an avid reader with a critical eye and I was worried that I would have to choose between hurting my friend with bad news or giving him false hopes. I feel that most of us have been in that situation at one time or another. So that same day I started on the book after dinner with my family, and it's the only thing I did until it was finished. When I was done, I was a mess of emotions. Shocked and pleased at how good it was. Grateful for the level of trust and sharing. Honored to be asked to be his editor. Jealous because

I've always wanted to be a writer. I did a lot of thinking on that last point and I've had a revelation about it. They say that you are a leader if you have followers. B.A. Bellec is a writer because he writes.

Someone's Story really spoke to me. We all have our journey, full of trials and tribulations. We all want things to end well, but we struggle with uncertainty and self-esteem. Even though I am far along as an adult, I don't know how things will end and it causes anxiety. It's even harder for a young person because so much is changing and they are still new to this journey we call life. If I could give advice, I would say to talk to yourself like you would talk to a friend. If you make a mistake - as we all do - it's not about self-blame, but helping to pick yourself up and dust yourself off. Failure is the first step to success. But the best advice I could probably give you is this: If you meet a smart, capable, loner weirdo – you should befriend them.

Sheila Harris

Editor

Determination

WHITE snow, two feet deep, as far as the eye can see. Cutting right through the middle is a small, cleared path. It's straight as an arrow into the horizon. Along the path are little orange flags every five hundred metres or so. You can only see a few of them as they are quite small.

Off in the distance, a black dot. A big exhale. The hot air billows out against the blue, icy winter sky. Steam follows a man like a vapour trail. The snow is crunching under the force of his electric yellow shoes, and the pace is like a metronome, always on point and never missing a beat.

Crunch.

        Crunch.

                Crunch.

        Crunch.

Exhale.

Someone's Story

Crunch.

Crunch.

Crunch.

Crunch.

Inhale.

The man is slender, but you can barely tell under what looks like three layers of clothes and a balaclava. All black except for the electric yellow gloves and armband, to match the shoes, of course. His facial hair is slightly overgrown. Not a beard but rather a long stubble. Adorning his chest is a giant eighty-eight on a square that looks pinned on.

Strangely, his eyes shut for two or three steps at a time, then open slowly. His feet are moving furiously, but he is completely relaxed, almost meditative. The black dot on the horizon is now more visible. It's another runner, and the gap shrinks with every step.

With a flurry of energy, the pace quickens and his stride lengthens. The black dot is now right in front of him. A few quick jump steps and it is as if the other runner was frozen in place by the frigid winter air.

A glance back reveals someone fading and a vast white plain of snow. Nothing else. No other black dots. Alone again, just the way he likes it. His pace slows back to his metronome, and his mind fades away to another place.

Crunch.

        Crunch.

                Crunch.

        Crunch.

Exhale.

        Crunch.

                Crunch.

        Crunch.

Crunch.

        Inhale.

Small Town

IT'S cold. That means different things to different
people. To be specific, I haven't seen the grass in
four months. When the wind gusts, my skin burns.
That part isn't so bad. The part that's horrible is the
wind is kicking up frozen snow and it feels like a
person is throwing a handful of razor blades at me. If
I don't dress properly, I would be lucky to survive
fifteen minutes. Like actually die. It's cold.

The sidewalks disappeared long ago, so I have to
brave the road for the short walk to school. It's
dangerous on these small-town roads. Sometimes, the
snow is blowing so hard I can't see more than a few
feet. Scary.

When I get to the front door, no one is there. The
building is small, so I can see all the way around to
the lot behind it. There are a few cars. On a good day,
we get twenty. I try my luck around back. The door is
unlocked. Once I get in, it looks like a ghost town. I
check all the rooms. Not a soul. This place is eerie
and unsettling. Maybe it's the prison bars on the
windows and the ketchup-themed school colours.

Eventually, in the lunchroom, I find a few of the teachers. As I walk in, I take notice of the room right next to the lounge. It is the tiniest office ever. It's more like a broom closet. Dr. Drum is written on the door. Funny name.

Teacher: Class is cancelled. Go home.

The teacher looks again and realizes it is me.

Teacher: How are you feeling? Is anyone bothering you?

They're always asking questions like that. I don't answer. Just sigh because I don't want to brave these conditions again, but I have no other choice. I slowly make my way along the country road back home, occasionally having to put my back to the wind or tuck my head deep into my chest in order to avoid the searing pain.

To my surprise, Dad's truck is back. Once I get inside, it takes a good five minutes until the feeling in my hands comes back and my clothing has thawed enough that I can take the first few layers off. Dad is sitting at the table.

Dad: Hey kiddo, we need to talk.

Instead of responding, I just make my way to the table and seat myself.

Dad: They're transferring me.

My eyebrows raise but I am too young and naive to really understand what that means.

> **Dad:** They offered me a good raise in a new position. But we have to move. I didn't want to take it. I looked around. My field is declining. There is nothing local. I am lucky they offered me what they did.

My mind races.

> **Someone:** I want to stay.

> **Dad:** No, we just can't.

> **Someone:** What about my mom?

> **Dad:** You know I don't know where she is.

> **Someone:** I'll find her.

> **Dad:** That's not a good idea.

I can hear the clock slowing, but at the same time my heart speeds up. Slower and faster, slower and faster. What is happening? I can't breathe. I need a drink. I can't move. Why can't I move? WHAT'S GOING ON?! The room spins and I fade to black.

A First Encounter

HE had recommended Starbucks. After a few
minutes on Google, I had a different
suggestion. It's Monday morning. The weather
is perfect. Everyone said this place has near-perfect
weather, except when it rains. I don't care about the
weather.

One of the benefits of moving, Dad gave me his old
car. It was a piece of junk, but at least I could get
myself around now. This city was so much bigger. At
least twenty times the population. I was still getting
my bearings.

When I pull up to the coffee shop, I like what I see.
Two blocks over is a Starbucks with people lined up
to the door. At least ten. Where I am though, this
shop is full of character. Stylish art. Nothing modern
about it. It looks old, but in a good way. There are
fifteen or so tables, and maybe five in use. One other
person getting a drink. My kind of joint.

I sit in the corner. I always go straight for the corner.
That's the wallflower in me. I want to be able to see
as much as I can. The coffee, blonde roast, no cream,

no sugar. If they don't have blonde, they don't have my business. I am fascinated by everyone's desire to drink burnt beans. The blonde roast is subtle, soft, light. A hybrid between coffee and tea almost. I remember the first day I found blonde roast. It was special. A few sips in and the world literally melted away. It was just my taste buds and that blonde roast. Every other coffee up until that moment had been okay unless blasted with copious amounts of cream. But the blonde roast, it didn't need sugar or cream. It had balance.

You're thinking, wait, he is seventeen, how much coffee has this seventeen-year-old even had? Fair question. I was a pretty straight arrow. Barely ever touched drugs or alcohol, but at fourteen, I tried my first coffee. It wasn't love at first sip though. I made my way around the various chains, slowly picking apart their menus. After about two years I found blonde roast, and it has become a staple. Maybe all the caffeine is part of my anxiety. The doctor told me to stop. I stopped for two weeks.

Here I am, sitting in the corner. I have my phone out. I am checking showtimes at the movie theatre when this guy walks in. Remember that reality show *Survivor*? I am a bit of a *Survivor* geek. Anyways, there was this one contestant named Rupert. He was a bit overweight, and he had a giant beard. He kind of looked like a pirate. His trademark was his tie-dye t-shirt. Do you know what Rupert's job was? Guidance counsellor for troubled teens.

So here comes this guy into the coffee shop. He looks like he could be brothers with Rupert, except he has a lean build and his hair is up in a bun. The thought crosses my mind, is this the guy, but there is no way. Just a coincidence. Then my phone vibrates and I look down. A text from the counsellor. He is here. I text back. Sure enough. The Rupert twin walks up to me.

I don't know what to think. This isn't what I expected at all. I thought it would be somebody a little more formal, like Dad.

He starts the conversation.

> **Man:** Hey, you bought a drink already. They're always on me.

> **Someone:** Oh, sorry, I didn't know.

> **Man:** Give me a second.

He walks up to the counter and orders a large dark roast coffee. I roll my eyes, but I am not giving him my rant on the first visit. No chance. I am already debating if I bring up *Survivor* or not.

He walks back and hands me two dollars.

> **Man:** There you go, buddy.

> **Someone:** Thanks...

I don't love the use of buddy there. I barely know you. Slow it down.

> **Man:** I'm Kevin. Nice to meet you.

9

He reaches out and shakes my hand. Firm, but not overpowering.

> **Man:** I'm gonna level with you. Most of the students that come through my door are either pregnant or a burnout, so I was excited for a change. I could tell you were different based on your dad.

> **Someone:** I didn't know you talked to Dad.

> **Kevin:** I did. He wanted to do everything to help. I like to customize my plans for each student. Usually, the students are already in our school, so I just ask the faculty. Your dad pulled all the strings. You are lucky. Lots of kids don't have that.

> **Someone:** He always does the right thing, that's Dad.

Kevin reaches down and sips his coffee. I watch his eyes, trying to read if he really likes that dark roast. Does he cringe at the bitterness? He doesn't. Maybe I can convert him though. In time. In time...

> **Kevin:** Why are you here?

Why am I here? There isn't one answer. Life isn't always as simple as cause and effect. We can get technical, and yes, I can tell him the inciting incident as to why I am currently here, but what I hate about society is its desire to treat symptoms instead of problems. If I only tell him why I am here with no backstory, it is just a snapshot. Please don't judge me based on a snapshot of my worst moment.

Someone: It's a long story.

Kevin: No judging.

Someone: I was born in a small town. I was raised in a small town. I thought I was going to spend most of my life in a small town. Where is my mom? My parents split up when I was five. Dad had the pleasure of winning the custody battle. At five, we started our new life in a slightly less small town. Dad has a good job. Twenty years at the same place, pension and benefits. The typical nineties career path. I don't know exactly what he does. What I know is he works at a desk and he works for the government. He keeps it private.

I look at Kevin to gauge his interest.

Someone: My mom. She is gone. When I say gone, I mean gone. I have no idea where she is. Maybe Dad does, but he doesn't share. If I had to guess, I would say she is probably on welfare renting a small apartment with some guy who shares her similar desire of avoiding responsibility. You may think I hate my mom, but I actually kind of respect her "not my problem" attitude. I know it is one of the reasons I struggle, but at the same time, I feel it inside me. So if she stuck to her guns through the years, props. I could have a coffee with her one day and talk about all the responsibilities we have ducked. Don't get me wrong. I love Dad, but I couldn't do what he does. Twelve years of just me and him. Twenty years at the same job. He did the right thing. Money isn't really a problem. More of an afterthought. We live a modest, middle-class lifestyle, and we don't indulge in things we can't afford. My social life wasn't great. Most of the kids picked on me. I was never on the inside. I had friends but none of them were deep connections. I just floated around really. Just Dad and me, feeling kind of trapped.

Kevin: And the incident?

Someone: I don't really remember it. I have this thing that happens where I pass out. When I come back, I barely remember the few hours leading into it. Those last few years, they are all a big blur. Dad tells me there have been others, but I just can't remember them well. After my most recent fall, I woke up in a hospital with a nice bandage on my head, a bottle of fancy pills that I couldn't spell if I tried, and a beautiful new anxiety diagnosis.

I am looking for a response. He is calculating. Processing. I see the gears turning. He is looking at me but also lost deep in thought.

Kevin: Honestly…

He pauses for a few seconds.

Someone: Go on.

Kevin: Honestly, I think you need to relax more. You are still young. You're moving fast. Slow down and enjoy the time for what it is. You can't predict the future. You can plan for it, but actually predicting, that is impossible. Set small goals. Achieve them. Stop and enjoy what is happening around you.

I was expecting more. Relax. Anyone can relax. That isn't advice. Do I take him seriously? Right now I am half expecting someone else to walk through the door and save me from the local serial killer. What the heck is going on?

He reaches down and gives his coffee another big gulp. I look down. I was halfway through before he came, and I haven't touched it since. I have been captivated. I finish off the last bit in two quick gulps.

Kevin: What do you do for exercise?

Someone: Exercise?

Kevin: You play any sports?

Someone: No.

Kevin: What about hobbies?

Someone: Video games...movies.

13

Kevin: You ever think of an active hobby?

Someone: No.

Kevin: I have a suggestion.

I am puzzled and intrigued, but don't give him an answer. I just raise an eyebrow back in his direction.

Kevin: Have you ever thought about jogging?

Someone: Hell no.

Kevin: It's a fantastic exercise. Really clears out the mind. Builds a mental toughness.

Someone: I guess. I don't know.

Kevin: Your dad did tell me one other thing.

Someone: What?

Kevin: He mentioned you like Survivor.

I knew it! A wardrobe choice like that couldn't have been an accident. Kevin gave a giant smile and we shared another couple of seconds together. He stands up, his tie-dye on display. He nods his head and says goodbye. That was weird. I am not accustomed to adults like this. They don't exist where I come from.

Inception

SATURDAY morning. Toast with Dad. We are still unpacking, so boxes are everywhere. Dad has always been quiet and reserved. Getting him to talk about feelings is near impossible. The one thing we can talk about for hours is movies.

> **Dad:** Kiddo, let's pause the packing. I've got a different plan.

> **Someone:** K.

He was reading the paper. He drops it on the table. It reveals the movie schedule. We used to drive forty-five minutes to get to a small three-screen theatre. The floors were sticky. The seats were falling apart. The place hadn't seen a dollar of maintenance in three years. Still, it was the only option when we wanted to see a big movie and the popcorn was alright. We look at each other.

> **Dad/Someone:** Inception.

We are both movie fans. *Inception* looks like a great one. Christopher Nolan reinvented the superhero film with *Batman Begins* and then forever changed the world with *The Dark Knight*. The haunting, layered performance by Heath Ledger will go down as one of the greatest in cinematic history, only made even more chilling by his untimely passing. In between the Batman movies, Nolan had made *The Prestige* about duelling magicians with escalating levels of madness. It had flaws. The Christian Bale character made some questionable decisions. Not nearly as famous or commercially successful, but worth the watch.

This is Nolan's much-anticipated follow-up to *The Dark Knight*. Leonardo DiCaprio headlines an all-star cast, and the trailers look mind-bending with city blocks folding onto each other and something to do with layered dreams.

An aside. I have been driving for almost a year. Driving where we came from, no big deal. There were maybe ten lights in the whole town. Pedestrians were scarce. Most of the time you could see deep into the horizon because it was flat farmland as far as you could see.

Driving in the city is different. It's terrifying at times. No one goes the speed limit. Stop signs seem to be optional. You have to watch for people on bikes going way too fast for people on bikes. Then the pedestrians. They walk around like they own the place. At any moment, one could emerge from behind anything. On top of all that, there are all kinds of roads and signs I have never seen before. Six lanes. Dedicated turning. U-turn lanes. I haven't even driven in rush-hour yet, usually sticking to early weekends when the roads are quiet and safe.

On the way, Dad gets me to make a quick stop at the drug store. He has to run in because I need my prescription. I haven't told him this, but I have been flushing them. Anyways, while he is inside, I admire the hustle and bustle of the city. Cars and people never stop. The churn and diversity are impressive to my simple upbringing. Before I even know it, he's back, and he brought a gift. When he gets in the car, he just hands it over. No pleasantries. I guess it is a house warming present. So Dad. It looks pretty cool. A moon lamp. Probably an impulse buy while he was waiting in line, but I think I am going to like it. He seems to have a few other things as well. I don't ask, but it is more than just my medicine.

My eyes light up as we drive up to the colossal structure. It is a hundred feet tall and wide as a city block. Giant posters for upcoming releases are plastered on the outside walls. The stairs up are grand. The entrance is glass from floor to ceiling, revealing at least ten cash registers to buy tickets and so many food options your mind spins. Five or six popcorn registers, but it doesn't stop there. French fries, burgers, pizza, ice cream. You can get anything.

There must be fifteen screens in the building. The hallways go for a half-mile, and digital signs hang from the ceiling, flashing current movies and showtimes.

Once we make our way through the army of people to get ourselves popcorn, we head to our theatre. We leave one hallway only to enter another. It's a good sixty feet until we actually enter the seating area.

Elevated rows on rows. Big wide chairs. Cupholders. A bit of a recline. This is amazing.

As for the movie. A two-and-a-half hour trip of mind-bending glory. Top-level sound, story, acting, and cinematography. Another Nolan classic and a good day with Dad.

The First Jog

DAD is gone to work. I have most of the unpacking for the day done. The new place is coming together. It's a two-bedroom rancher. Dad, he lives within his means, and he picked just enough space for two people to share. Right about now is when I would turn to television or video games, but today is a new day in a new place, and I have a new goal: jog!

Old red Nike runners. A black headband. My best light clothing. I loop the laces together. I am excited to give this a try. I start by stretching. I think you are supposed to be loose. I don't know what I am doing though.

Outside I go. I decide to keep it close to home. Run around the block a few times. I start. I hop into my first stride. I keep my arms tight. I watched a video and they said part of jogging is the efficiency of movement. You don't want to flail around too much.

One foot goes in front of the other. This isn't too bad. Not pushing myself hard. Just keep those feet moving. Watch for cars. Watch for uneven ground. Focus. Lift my knees more.

I am two blocks in. Pick up the pace a little. My lungs can feel it. It kind of burns. It doesn't really hurt though. It's a good burn.

Wow, I am sweating everywhere. It feels weird. Almost euphoric. The sweat leaving my body tingles and burns, but there is no pain.

Eight blocks in. My lungs are on fire. My skin is on fire. But it isn't an uncontrolled fire. I am controlling the fire. I am covered in flames, but I am at peace. The Human Torch.

Getting close to home. My thighs and calves are starting to feel it. The skin and lung burning is gone. Now all I feel are my legs. It's not pain. It's more of a tingle. I am aware something is happening but it's not enough to stop. It's just a new feeling.

I run past the house, going for another lap. Let's see if I can do it faster. I hit this zen-like state of concentration. There is a checklist that my brain is processing with each step:

Inhale.

Fists tight.

Arms in.

Look for uneven ground.

Look for vehicles and obstacles.

Lift your other foot and move it forward.

Exhale.

Repeat.

Over and over I do this. Life just falls away. For thirty minutes I feel something new and different. I have run before, but never like this. It was always half-trying gym laps against my will. This time I am pressing myself. I feel the release.

When I arrive home from the second lap, I am soaked in sweat. My headband is dripping. My shirt is stuck to my back. It's like I was running in the rain. I get my clothes off. Turn on the shower. I step in. This is when I feel the pain.

My nipples sting as if they have been cut off.

I look down and realize they are bleeding. What the hell happened? I cover them with my hands and try to shower off as sheltered as I can.

The Expanding Mind

ONE week since our first meeting. I have a jog under my belt, and I feel at ease. Sure enough, a P.T. Cruiser pulls up to Brown Bean. The man bun pops out. He signals me over to the door. We order. I go first.

> **Someone:** One blonde roast. No sugar or cream.

Then it happens. He utters words that put an ear-to-ear grin on my face.

> **Kevin:** I'll have the same.

Success! Once they try it, they never go back.

> **Kevin:** Why are you smiling?

> **Someone:** You are trying my drink.

> **Kevin:** And that makes you happy?

Someone: It does. I feel good. You have no idea what you are about to taste, do you?

Kevin: Nope. I have never had anything except regular or dark. It's what all the teachers drink.

Someone: I got a question. What's the deal with the car?

Kevin: Old P.T.?

Someone: Sure.

Is that what he calls it?

Kevin: It was a gift from my parents. The best car is a free car that runs. It has some sentimental value, so I just can't seem to let it go.

We make our way to our spot. I sit in my corner. We grab our cups. I smell mine. Savouring the moment. You only get one first time with a blonde roast, and watching someone else have their first time is like a window into the past. The cleaner aroma. The lighter colour. The subtle flavour. He picks up his cup and slowly raises it to his mouth. His eyes are closed. He is channelling his senses to his taste buds. My eyes are locked on his eyes with anticipation. There it is. His eyes open up wide. He tastes it and loves it. Woody. Nutty. Soft, but still coffee. I can't contain my joy!

Someone: Every coffee bean you tasted up until right now has been burnt. That is the true flavour of coffee in all its glory.

He nods his head. I have converted another. He responds with a question.

Kevin: So, did you jog?

Someone: I did.

Kevin: And?

Someone: In the moment, it felt great. I thoroughly enjoyed it. It was after the jog when I had some not so pleasant events.

Kevin: Elaborate.

Someone: Well, first was my nipples. When I stepped into the shower, it was like someone had cut my nipples off. When I looked down, I noticed they were bleeding.

He laughs.

Kevin: Jogger's nipple, really? On the first run?

He laughs again.

Kevin: Well, it's pretty common. Don't freak. Just use protection next time.

I smile. The pain actually doesn't bother me that much, and I like that it brought Kevin some entertainment.

Kevin: Anything else?

Someone: The next morning, my legs felt like they were turning to stone. I could barely bend my joints.

Kevin: That is muscle forming. With leg pain. It usually goes away after a day or so. That is just the body tearing and rebuilding muscle. If the pain doesn't go away, or if it feels different than normal, then you see the doctor because that is joint pain. Also, protein is good. Don't forget to stretch. Ten to fifteen minutes. I will get you a few easy starter exercises. Make sure to stretch after too. Good shoes are super important.

Someone: You know a lot about jogging.

Kevin: I run half marathons four or five times each year. Last time, I finished in the top five for my age bracket. Jogging is one of the best decisions I ever made.

We share a moment. He gave me something, jogging, and I gave him something, blonde roast.

Kevin: Any anxiety? You seem to be in a good place.

Someone: I do feel good, but the strange thing is I felt good right up until I woke up in a hospital. I don't know how I will handle another incident.

Kevin: Exercise and writing can be a fantastic way to keep anxiety at bay. Start a journal.

A journal? Am I an eight-year-old girl?

Kevin: Writing is really good for the soul. Don't laugh at it until you try. It helps get issues out of you, and they become easier to talk about.

Hmmmm....

Kevin: What is your social life like? You have been here a few weeks.

Someone: Honestly, it's just me and Dad. I have talked to my old friends online, but it feels weird.

Kevin: And me.

We smile.

Kevin: What do you mean weird?

Someone: I am not a huge social media fan. I like in-person. Face-to-face. You really get to know someone that way. It's faster. You read off them. Online feels detached, and I don't like it. I also had some trouble back home. A few kids kept bothering me.

Kevin: Interesting. Did you address it?

Someone: It's complicated.

And I don't want to talk about it yet…

Kevin: What are you doing to try and find friends?

Someone: Nothing. Just waiting for school.

Kevin: It's a big world. You can find people outside of school.

Someone: I don't really do that.

Kevin: I think you should try. I have another idea.

Someone: I'm listening.

Kevin: I have a friend. He is like me. Younger guy. Asian. Good sense of humour. He runs one of the local pizza shops, and I know he needs a part-time driver right now. He loves hiring high school kids.

Someone: A job?

Kevin: Yes, a job. I don't think it would be the worst way to spend the rest of your summer. I know there are some other young people on the staff. Put some money in your pocket for when the school year starts.

Someone: Dad doesn't want me to work.

Kevin: Talk to him again. I think this is a great idea. If you like me, you will like this place. Trust me.

I am giving it some thought.

The Pizza Game

I honestly don't know how working in a small town would have gone. I was a little ball of anxiety. There were barely any jobs. My mind wasn't ready.

My budding jogging hobby is turning into a daily ritual. The muscle soreness is not carrying over into the next day. I have found the pace and distance that my body can handle. Life is good.

I roll up to the pizza shop ten minutes early, and there she is. Her hair is dyed with bright red streaks to match the Bambino's uniform. Her makeup is subtle, a bit of white foundation to accent her gothic vibe. Red lipstick to match the hair and uniform. She has a nose ring. Nothing overpowering. More than a few tattoos are making their way out from under her shirt onto what you can see of her collarbone and wrists.

I am in my car. I just take another few seconds to observe. She isn't wearing jeans. I think they're black yoga pants. They are way too tight.

Eventually, I make my way to the door. I am
paralyzed. What do I say? I can barely look at her.
Then it happens. This soft, angelic voice comes out.

Samantha: Hey. You have a name?

Did she just talk to me? That doesn't happen. She
must not know who I am. How do I keep it that way?
If she finds out anything about me, there is no way
she would talk to me. Play it cool. Just like in the
movies. Wait, this is just like in the movies because I
feel like I might pass out, and I haven't felt like this
about a person before. Keep it together.

Someone: Just call me Someone.

She looks at me, kind of confused.

Samantha: Whatever. Is that your car?

She looks over at my black Volkswagen Golf. The
plastic has started to fade to grey. The front bumper
has a nice hole in it.

Someone: It is.

Samantha: Better than nothing, I guess.
What's that?

She points down at the hole in the bumper.

Someone: That's my bird hole.

She immediately bursts out with laughter.

B.A. Bellec

Samantha: Tell me more.

Someone: The other day I was driving, and I hit a bird. It left a hole. Hence, bird hole.

Samantha: You are kind of weird, but in a good way.

She stops and looks at me again before moving on.

Samantha: Hey, you coming?

Dork move number one. I am frozen in place. Three feet outside the door and lost in my mind. Great start.

Samantha: What grade you in?

Someone: Twelve.

Samantha: Me too. You just move here? I know most of the kids in our grade.

Someone: Yup. Two weeks.

Samantha: Where were you from before that?

Someone: Nowhere special.

Her cheeks lift up with a smirk, and a small casual chuckle comes out. Did my stupid joke just make her laugh? Play it cool. My heart and mind are racing, but my body is frozen.

31

We continue to talk about our parents for the next little bit. Her mom works in a diner, and her dad is not around. She also talks about her brother, Caleb. They are twins so they both are in the same grade. The three of them live in a trailer park not far from the shop. He works here too. They don't talk lots, though, outside work. For the first time in my life, a girl I like is talking to me like I exist. Crazy!

The phone rings. It's order number one. She pulls her hair back and ties it high. The red streaks are still clearly visible. I observe from afar as she pulls the dough out and works it with her hands. A quick toss in the air. The perfect pizza.

> **Samantha:** I know first days can be hard. This place is pretty chill. The owner is super cool. A younger guy named Toni.

> **Someone:** Neat.

I am such a dork. Neat. Who says neat? The next seven hours fly by. Apparently, this is a slow night, but it doesn't go slowly for me. Even though she said to just run the oven, I am jumping all over the place. Helping anywhere I can. I take a phone call. Learn the deals. Top a few pizzas. I navigate my GPS like Columbus discovering the new world. It is easily one of the most exciting nights of my life to date. When all is said and done, I believe I did fifteen deliveries and totalled north of a hundred dollars to take home. Around ten, she shuts off the sign, then oven. I have one last job, dishes, and then I'm free to go.

There was another driver on the shift as well. I honestly barely even remember talking to him. I was in a trance, just trying not to spoil the moment.

Growth Spurt

MY last face-to-face meeting with the counsellor before the school year because he is going away for the last month of summer. By the time Kevin sits down, he has already ordered the drinks. Obviously, my work converting him, now complete. No questions asked, blonde roast with nothing extra. Today's attire is the stylish black cargo shorts and red polo combo accented with Ray-Ban Aviators.

Kevin: How goes it with work?

Someone: Man. Thanks. I love the job. It's been a blast.

Kevin: How many shifts in?

Someone: Just two.

Kevin: I thought you would. Keep it up. Toni is a cool guy. We go way back. And the jogging? How goes that?

Someone: I am trying to run every day. Found a good distance and pace where I am not getting sore. Happy to report my nipples are in great shape.

He chuckles.

Kevin: You tracking them?

Someone: My nipples?

We both laugh.

Someone: Nope.

Kevin: Get an app. You can compete with yourself and see how much better you get. Do you know where I am going?

Someone: Away.

Kevin: Way away. I am competing in a triathlon in Hawaii. All summer I have been gradually increasing my distance. I think I could win this one.

Someone: Good luck!

Kevin: I don't like luck. Luck is kind of a factor, but most of the time it comes down to drive and preparation.

I actually agree with him completely. I just said it because it felt like the socially normal thing to say.

Kevin: So how is friend life?

Someone: I only met Toni and...what's her name?

I pretend I can't remember, but believe me, I remember her name.

Kevin: I don't know his staff too well. I know she goes to our school. I think her name is Samantha? Is she cool?

Someone: We didn't really talk much, so I don't know.

Another lie. We talked enough that I know she is cooler than me.

Kevin: Well, keep it up. You are doing great. I want you to write and jog as often as you can while I am gone. Between the jogging, writing, and work, I really think you are going to do great going into senior year. Have you given post-secondary any thought?

Someone: A little. I think I might want to be a writer.

Kevin: How are your marks in English?

Someone: Okay, but I haven't been trying that hard. I think I can do better if I focus, and take a few courses that go well with

English. History. Art. I feel they have good symmetry.

Kevin: I think you are right on track. By the time I get back, it will be the start of school. Our next meeting will be in my office. It's a lot to take in, so if you start to feel anxious, remember to write, run, and talk to me. We can get you through this.

Someone: Do you mind if I ask a personal question?

Kevin: Sure.

Someone: What does that tattoo mean? "Not Done"?

He pulls up his sleeve a little to reveal the tattoo on the bottom of his wrist.

Kevin: I got that when I got married. It's a reminder. Every time I have a bad thought or think about quitting. Whether it's regarding a project at home, a run, a fight we are having. I look down and I remember I can do better.

Someone: What's your family like?

Kevin: My wife and I are best friends. She runs with me. We have a daughter who is eleven. She is off at summer camp right now. It's great.

Someone: Where did you meet her?

Kevin: University. I was studying in my second year. I took a lot of general studies in my first few years. It was a psychology class. We got assigned to work together. She liked studying the mind and I had a messy one, so I let her in. We really hit it off on that project. If my memory serves me right, we did pretty badly on the project because we spent all the time talking.

The end of my summer counselling. I can't believe how much change has happened in just a couple of months. I am starting to feel like an adult. It is pulsing through my veins. Two months ago, I was a scared child, but that person is just a distant memory.

The next month flys by. Samantha's twin brother, you wouldn't know they were twins if they stood next to each other. He is a tall, spindly fellow. Pretty clean cut. He just seems inviting. Like he just wants to fit in. It's something I recognize quickly in mannerisms and the first few words of dialogue they speak because I have it too. I didn't want to talk to Caleb about Samantha. It took about three minutes until we found our topic of conversation. Movies and TV. We spend most of the next few weeks discussing the various shows we grew up on.

Another highlight was my next shift with Samantha. It was a Wednesday night with just me and her. When I get there, she has already unlocked the store and everything is set up. I come in, and she is in the back office working on the computer doing admin stuff. I slither my way to the back.

Someone: Morning.

I am such a dope. It isn't morning. Why am I so inept at social situations? She smiles though.

Samantha: It's morning somewhere.

She didn't have her uniform on yet. She is wearing a summer top that exposed both of her shoulders. I can see her tattoo in all its glory. It's a dragon.

Someone: Is that a dragon?

Samantha: Dragons are so strong and cool. I love them.

Luck…is it real? For the first time in my life, I caught a lucky break, and I mean that luck is a factor through and through. You see, on this particular night it is extremely slow and we get to talk.

Someone: What do you watch?

Samantha: I don't watch much TV. Caleb got me into anime.

Someone: I never watched any, except for Dragon Ball Z.

Samantha: Which others do you know?

Someone's Story

Someone: Is Pokémon anime?

Samantha: Sure, but that's a kid's show.
What about Akira, Ghost in the Shell,
Cowboy Bebop, Trigun, Spirited Away,
Princess Mononoke, Hell Girl?

I return a blank stare.

Samantha: Those are the ones you should
watch. Not Pokémon. Don't get me wrong.
Pokémon is good, but it's like the Sesame
Street of anime. Try some real stuff.

Eventually, we move to family and I explain
everything I remember about my mom and dad. She
chimes in with some more insights about hers. Her
mom is pretty broke. They get child support from
their dad, sometimes. Samantha and Caleb have to
work. Their mom just doesn't have the extra cash.
We also talk about Caleb. I never had any siblings so
I was learning about what it is like to have a sibling.
Samantha was torn between wanting out of the trailer
park and needing to help her mom.

After the first hour of no action, I take a delivery.
When I get back, I move the conversation to work.
We talk about stupid customers. She tells me a few
unbelievable stories from other drivers. She gets into
inventory and ordering products. She is just a wealth
of knowledge. It is her second year here already.

A few more deliveries come and go. Then we get to
our main event. What does any seventeen-year-old
have? Dreams. Big ones. The entire world is theirs. I

push her to go first. She says she was hoping to go to college and study art history with plans of maybe becoming a tattoo artist in a major city one day. Money is a factor. She will be paying for everything entirely by herself and it may come down to delaying her plans to provide for the family.

That is so cool. Of course, she has a cool life plan. My life plan up until two months ago was wake up tomorrow, but I have a better plan now. My plan is relatively new though, and I haven't put thought into where I would go to become a writer, but, none-the-less, we burn another hour going back and forth discussing my budding career aspiration.

If I had recorded that night, I am sure I could have lit a dark room with the electricity coming off us. I remember the end of the night. It was about ten-thirty. I had done the dishes and floors. In her soft angelic voice, she says exactly what I want to hear.

> **Samantha:** Shitty we had a slow night. You probably only made seventy bucks, but it was fun talking.
>
> **Someone:** It's all good.
>
> **Samantha:** Do you want to give me a lift home? The driver usually does.
>
> **Someone:** Of course.

I spend at least an hour lying on my bed looking up at the ceiling. Everything has gone perfectly. She knows just enough about me to be curious still. I know more about her than any girl I have ever talked with. I feel like I am floating. It didn't matter I had only made seventy dollars. I feel rich.

Sometimes, feelings can be complicated though. It is almost the last shift of the summer. I have been coasting. Everything feels perfect. Caleb and I are growing a friendship. Samantha is still talking to me. I am starting to fit in. I even bought Samantha a black long sleeve t-shirt with a montage of the Studio Ghibli films. She loved it.

Then, it happens. A delivery truck backs up to the door. Out pops the driver. He looks well over twenty. Wears trendy glasses. Short black hair spiked off to the side slightly. A nicely groomed black beard. Maybe an inch long and manly thick. Taller than me, and more slender. I wouldn't call him buff, but he isn't skinny either. He is a grown man; I am still a teenager. He unloads the supplies. Flour, mushrooms, green peppers, pepperoni, tomatoes, and anything else you might expect a pizza shop to use.

I didn't notice, but Samantha has left the shop. She walks over to him. I expect her to grab an invoice or something. Nope. She jumps up and hugs him. My heart sinks. You see, the question I forgot to ask, maybe out of fear, maybe out of not wanting to know, the question was really simple: was Samantha single? I just got my answer.

I walk over to Caleb, who is munching on some customer's rejected pizza, and give him a nudge to look over to the door.

Someone: Who is that?

Caleb: That is Josh.

Someone: And who is Josh?

Caleb: Josh is a few things. He delivers our supplies, he dates Samantha, and he is a slimy, disgusting human being.

I have never heard Caleb say something like that about anyone yet. It gives me a little bit of hope.

Someone: What?

Caleb: Samantha had a boyfriend for two years. When they broke up, which was around the end of the school year, Josh swooped in like a vulture. I think he has a kid already with someone else, and I am not privy to the laws, but with the age gap, it's borderline rape. He makes me sick.

Someone: Does Samantha know about the kid?

Caleb: She won't really talk about it. Every time you try to bring up Josh, she changes the subject or leaves. It's taboo.

Someone: Does your mom know?

Caleb: No. Our mom is barely home, and Josh never comes around the house. I think

the words Samantha used were: If you tell
Mom about Josh, I'll kill you.

I don't respond. I am lost in my thoughts. Spinning
into myself. What am I supposed to do next?

Caleb: You still with me?

I snap back to reality. My mind had taken over. My
anxiety had crept back in. I was starting to spin, but
Caleb's voice found me.

Someone: Oh, sorry about that. You doing
anything tomorrow?

Caleb: No.

Someone: Awesome. I got something in
mind.

Determination: The Mountain

THE trail ahead is lit by a small, but powerful, headlamp. Luckily, there is also a full moon out. The snow reflects moonlight everywhere. It might be the middle of the night, but it's by no means dark.

Crunch.

                Crunch.

                                Crunch.

Crunch.

                Exhale.

                                Crunch.

                Crunch.

Crunch.

Someone's Story

Crunch.

Inhale.

This is strenuous and crazy. Each step is a few feet of elevation gained. This isn't walking. The pace is fast. Not running. Not hiking. A combination of everything. Not many people go all night.

Every now and then, a person is bundled up on the side. Wrapped in a foil blanket. Weak. Unable to proceed. Whatever it is: fatigue, temperature, darkness, will power. They stopped. Just keep moving. Don't stop. You can't stop. This is bigger than you. Use their weakness as fuel. Use your negative thoughts as fuel. Straight up the mountain in the middle of the night.

Crunch.

Crunch.

Crunch.

Crunch.

Exhale.

Crunch.

Crunch.

Crunch.

Crunch.

Inhale.

The pace never changes. The path always stays clear. The moon keeps guiding. Where others fall to the side, keep going. Stronger. Tougher. Faster. The mind races. It's okay.

Sleeping isn't even an option. Pure adrenaline. It would be impossible to stop now. The moon might as well be the sun as it lights up his eighty-eight.

Part insanity. Part savage. Not done. Don't stop. Things are only impossible if you get in your own way. Remove yourself from the equation. Find the truth. Be one with the truth. The truth is you can do this if you set your mind to it.

C.O.D.

DESPITE the fact that I view myself as a lone wolf, humans are social creatures. We need each other. You can only be alone for so long before it starts to get to you. I have adult friends: Dad and Kevin. But they are more like mentors. I want Samantha to be my friend badly, but I don't want to screw that up so I am happy to go slowly. My loneliness is starting to get to me. I had a few friends my age before. I have none now. Enter Caleb.

We have good chemistry. I had extended the invite for coffee at Brown Bean. He didn't hesitate to say yes. Between the few shifts we had worked, I was pretty sure Caleb could easily be my first true friend since the move. This coffee is going to be my test, if you will. How deep is he willing to go? Is he an acquaintance, like so many of the people in my previous life, or is he a friend?

As per usual, I am there first. Twenty minutes or so early. I order my blonde roast and just sit there in my corner looking out the window, pondering this first month. How everything is starting to feel like it is coming together.

Caleb shows up right on time. He was riding his bike. A nice mountain bike. Good suspension. Bright green colours. He locks it up near the door. When he comes in, I raise my cup up. He sees me and then lines up. He orders something ridiculous. Chai Matcha Decaf Latte with extra whip, I believe. Looking at it makes me a little queasy. He sits down. I usually don't bring up the blonde roast with coffee newbs. They don't appreciate it. You have to drink dark roast for at least a few months to appreciate all the subtlety of a blonde roast. Don't believe me? Try it. Drink a cup of dark roast every day for a month, then switch to blonde. You won't believe what you taste.

> **Someone:** I wanted to talk to you about school. I am new here. Can you take me under your wing, so to speak? Show me your friends. Show me around. Give me some hot spots. Places and people I should be avoiding. Teachers that students don't like. The whole gambit.

> **Caleb:** Cool. Ya. Ya. We can go over that stuff. Okay, so what is your favourite class?

> **Someone:** I don't know. English?

> **Caleb:** What? Why? Okay. Okay. There are a few English teachers. Ms. B is the one no one likes to get. She is super strict. No talking. Tough marker. A real troll. Think cat lady gone mad with power.

> **Someone:** Sounds like a real treat.

Caleb: I also recommend you sign up for Business Essentials. I have heard good things. Plus, it's a one-off, so we are guaranteed to be together. The teacher is supposed to be cool, and the class is fun. A few of the people who graduated last year said they actually learned something.

Caleb takes a sip of his drink. Or maybe it was a bite? I think he is drinking but he might be eating. I don't know what that thing he ordered was.

Caleb: Now, as for places. It's not the most cliquey school. Everyone kind of talks to everyone. Of course, the smokers have the parking lot. The jocks have the gym. Most people just hang in the hallways and the lunchroom.

Someone: I am a bit of a floater. I talk to everyone, but don't get close to many people.

Caleb: You'll do fine then. Just be the guy who comes to work every day. As for the people to avoid. We have a few kids, always getting suspended and fighting. The total rejects. You can see them from a mile away though. I will point them out. As for what is cool; casual and slightly retro dress. Flannel, hoodies, and jeans. Converse All-Stars. It's a fairly academic school. Most of the students are trying. It's almost cool to do well. Everyone spends most of the day on their phones. Sending messages back and forth.

Get used to using your phone all day. You
have an iPhone right?

Someone: No, my dad got me this shitty flip
thing.

Caleb: Get rid of that. They'll laugh you out
the door on day one. Go get yourself an
iPhone.

Someone: Can we go do that now?

Caleb: Sure. We can go check out the
school quick too. It will be locked, but we
can go around the outside.

Someone: Cool.

We mobilize. I put his bike in my trunk and bungee it
shut. We shuttle over to the mall. He shows me his
clothing stores, and then we pick up a phone. The guy
in the store doesn't want to sell me a phone at first
without my dad, but I happen to be holding eight
hundred dollars cash from being a baller pizza driver
so he agrees to sell it to me outright.

The mall is only about ten minutes from the high
school. When we get there, I am taken aback a little.
It's way bigger than what I am used to. Three stories.
Sprawling parking lot. It looks like thousands of kids
go here. The lot is closed, so we park on the road.
Caleb pulls his bike out and jumps on it. He takes me
around. Showing me where the smokers hang out.
Where the fields are outside. He takes me to the

outside of the cafeteria and shows me some of his spots through windows.

Along the tour, I ask about Samantha. I do it subtly, as if indulging him with a pleasantry. Where does she hang out? He says she is one of the more popular girls. He doesn't spend much time with her at school and doesn't really know where she hangs. Everyone knows they're twins, but they have their circles. Outside of the occasional class, they act like strangers to each other in school.

The school is sharply painted. Almost majestic in its detail, yet sleek in its design. There is pride. The fields are well-groomed. None of the paint lines in the parking lot are fading. The front entrance is sleek and modern. There are at least ten stairs leading up to it. The staircase is wide, at least one hundred feet.

Caleb also goes over the school app quickly. You get your schedule and all kinds of alerts right through the phone. After twenty minutes of going around the school, I ask him a question.

Someone: You doing anything tonight?

Caleb: No.

Someone: You game?

Caleb: COD?

Someone: Hell yes.

We jump in the car and drive back to my dad's place. It's Friday, so Dad is not home from work yet. I shoot him a text that I have a work friend over. He asks if we want pizza for dinner. We both work at a pizza shop so I let him know to get something else.

About forty-five minutes later, Dad shows up with Chinese. He watches us for a bit. We are playing *Call of Duty: Modern Warfare 2* Deathmatch online, taking turns. Caleb is good, but so am I. We're going for the nuke. Twenty-five kills in a row without dying. When I tell Dad we are going for the nuke, he knows what I mean and he goes from casual watching to intense focus.

We are all in the zone. Like comrades on the battlefield. Calling out movement. Radar beeps. Things in the sky. Anything to help. It isn't long before I get a good run going. I have the 50 Cal, and I am camping hard. Double claymores set up on the doors. Good vision from my window. I hit five or six from the window.

I hear a claymore explode. I don't get the kill, but it's my sign to hide. Quickly, I crouch and hit a corner behind a couch. Patience. Dad and Caleb are both shouting. I am calm and cool. As soon as the head peeks out from the stairs, I unload a magazine from my secondary Uzi. He falls and drops a bag. I pick it up and reset the claymore.

I eventually find my way to eleven kills and an AC-130. I hide well and take control of the bomber in the sky. I rain down huge blasts. Kill after kill. At least seven or eight deaths.

Now I am close. I am back on the battlefield trying to get my bearings when out of nowhere a grenade launcher blast lands square on me.

Dad and Caleb both cry out in disbelief. So close.

Another few games go. The food is mostly gone. Dad has been in and out, kind of waiting for action. Curious to see if we can do it.

Caleb is up. It's probably his sixth go. He is using the dual shotgun to start. It's total cheese, but anyone in close range is done.

He gets to seven kills so fast. Minutes. He is at eleven kills. Unbelievable. This is the run! Dad has taken notice and has returned to his role yelling at the TV. I am more silent, totally in the zone with Caleb.

The AC-130 comes, and within seconds, Caleb has landed a pair of double kills. The other team is fully exposed and stuck in a respawn trap. Caleb unloads shell after shell. Dad is yelling with excitement. I don't even know how many die. It might have been ten kills.

Now Caleb is being careful. He crouches and watches his corners. Using his ears. He is fast on the trigger. Whenever he hears or sees anything, they don't have a chance. His last few kills take almost half the time remaining in the match, but he isn't going to let this go.

The timer ticks down and the screen turns orange. The match ends instantly. This is a wonderful night for me, Caleb, and Dad.

The New School

EVERYONE remembers their first day at a new
school. It all moves so fast. So much to absorb
and navigate. If only the job was as simple as
show up, do your work, move on. It's not. Part of
school is getting a social education. Learning how to
network. Deal with people you don't see eye to eye
with. Assignments you don't want to do. If you
struggle socially, school is like a nightmare. You just
want to survive.

The first day is short. Just a meet and greet. Confirm
schedules and lockers. As per normal, I am early.
Way early. The school app has given me my classes
already. I receive most of what I wanted. The trouble
spot is English. Of course, Caleb said to watch out for
Ms. B, and, sure enough, I get Ms. B. I don't know
what that means but I know I want to do well.

My old school had five hundred students. This is a
complete overhaul of what I know school to be. The
sign hovering above the glass door out front is part
digital. It has rotating text of various events. Above
it, the school name: Riverside High. The lettering,
trendy. The sign looks to be pretty new, within the

last few years. I looked for the river earlier. It is
across the road but isn't much of a river. More of a
creek. The school colours, black and electric yellow. I
kid you not, the colour is called electric yellow. If I
had to describe my old school's feature colour, I
would call it old, off-brand ketchup. Electric yellow
is so in. I wonder how they came to that. Did the
students vote? Did Mountain Dew sponsor it?

There are little splashes of electric yellow
everywhere. The fire alarms, the occasional wall
stripe, random posters. Some buildings are pretty
easy to get around in. Not this one. It is intense and
rivals any mall I have ever been in. Lucky for me, the
app has a school map in it, so between the schedule
and the map, I am able to get around without too
much confusion. Still, it is stressful, seeing all these
new people and being in a new place.

Once I am inside, ten percent of the other students are
already navigating around. Most are like me,
confused-looking. See, I think it is pretty common to
arrive early when you are nervous. It gives you time
to acclimate and adjust. Most of these other early
arrivals are probably new students as well. Heads
buried in their phones, trying to find their way
around.

One of the first things I notice is how tech-savvy this
school is. They have Wi-Fi throughout. There are
dozens of screens in the hallways rotating similar text
to what is showing on the front of the building, as
well as what looks like student-produced ads for
various clubs and classes.

When I finally make my way to homeroom, I am still twenty minutes early. The door is open, but no one else is there. As soon as I enter, the lights turn on. There is also a digital projector. I noticed most of the rooms had one as I was navigating the halls earlier. The windows in each classroom are also modern. No prison bars like my old school.

I pick out a nice seat in the back corner. Just with the grade twelves, I believe I counted seven different homerooms, so the chances of me getting Caleb or Samantha are slim. Time ticks away and my anxiety pulses, wondering if anyone here will like me. Caleb and Samantha are nowhere to be found. Eighty percent full. A steady dose of jeans and hoodies.

A girl sits down in front of me and then turns around. She doesn't stop talking. It's relentless. I think she tells me her entire summer down to the tiniest detail of which cereal, on which day, and the whole time she barely pauses to let me get a word in. She is new here too. She went to Disneyland. I think I retain five percent of what she tells me.

Only half my attention is on the words. The other half is watching the door, curious who will come in. Hopeful for a familiar face, or at the very least, an inviting face. Just before the bell rings, and with maybe two seats left, a girl walks in. She has white headphones in. She doesn't look like she wants to be here. She travels light. No supplies. Her straight white shoulder-length hair has bangs to one side, covering one of her eyes slightly. Dressed in a white summer dress that borders on too short. She sits down next to me. She doesn't bother to take her headphones out or look around too much. I can sort of make out the music because it's fairly loud.

Shortly thereafter, our homeroom teacher comes in. He doesn't say much. Calls out attendance. Goes over the steps if we have a scheduling problem. Tells us how lockers are assigned and that we are to report back to homeroom again first thing tomorrow for one last check-in. Then he plays a ten-minute video over the projector about how awesome it is to be a senior at Riverside High.

We already had our lockers assigned when we got our schedule. I make my way over to mine. Right underneath me is the girl that wouldn't stop talking. Oh well. I hope she told me everything already.

The girl with the headphones. She never took them out the entire time. When homeroom was done, she just got up and left. Didn't say a word. Didn't check out her locker. She just vanished.

Caleb had said phones were important, and sure enough, almost every student has a phone surgically attached to their hand. I get a message from Caleb. He is done his homeroom, so I make my way over to the cafeteria to meet him.

Remember how I said this school is big? It takes me at least fifteen minutes to get to the cafeteria. Adding to it was that most of the students were now out in the hallways. The eerily quiet building of earlier had given way to a torrent of noise. High fives, giggles, and just general chatter made it nearly impossible to hear and navigate. Thousands of people catching up on two months, comparing schedules, complaining about teachers, talking summer flings. I crashed into a tall jock. He stared me down. I quickly apologized and went on my way.

I finally arrive at the cafeteria. It's closed for the day, but a few of the students wanting a quieter place have made their way over knowing it wouldn't be a mecca.

Here he is. The tall, spindly familiar friend. Next to him sits a small skinny fellow with short hair, bleached white, and multiple piercings. He kind of looks like a young Eminem. His name is Geoffrey. Both in hoodies and jeans. Most of all, the thing I notice and respect is they are not looking at their phones. They are not sharing photos or on social media. They are talking.

Across from them sits a girl. I'm stunned though. It's not just any girl. It's headphones girl. I didn't recognize her at first from across the cafeteria. Her white hair glows even more in the better light. Her headphones are no longer in.

Caleb waves me over. I catch a little bit of the conversation as I am walking, and it has something to do with how much they dislike being led around like all the other lemmings. Caleb is eating a bag of potato chips from a vending machine. He is always snacking on junk food but is skinny as a rail.

Strangely, the girl doesn't say much. Her words are chosen carefully. Light and precise, just like everything else about her. Her name is Ashley. Geoffrey and Caleb never shut up. They talk over each other, just like old friends. Caleb gives them my backstory, just a nobody from nowhere.

Counsellor's Office

THE buzzer sounds to indicate the start of homeroom. I, of course, am firmly planted in my corner. Curious where Ashley is, even though I have only known her for about twenty-four hours. Sure enough, just before the second bell, she floats in.

Everyone else has textbooks, binders, and bags. Not Ashley. I don't even think she has a pen. She has her headphones in again and is chewing gum. Once she sits down next to me, she removes one of her buds.

Ashley: Sup.

I am about to answer when the homeroom teacher arrives. I guess getting one bud out is progress. He tells us to check our schedules again for last-minute changes. He goes over the holidays, important grad dates, and a few other things. Somewhere near the end, Ashley manages to disappear, probably unnoticed by all. This might be her specialty.

After homeroom, we are released to the wolves to see if we will survive senior year of high school.

Strangely, I have managed a spare, and that spare happens to be my first block today, so my senior year is still on hold for another hour or so. None-the-less, I have a plan. Off to find Counsellor Kevin. It has been a month since I last saw him.

I wait for most of the hallways to declutter. Now, phone in hand, I navigate back to the offices near the front entrance. As I approach, I notice a pregnant girl leaving. There is a small entrance with a few chairs for waiting, and then two offices. One of the offices has things hanging everywhere. Papers stacked up. The other looks unused. No one else is here right now, but I figure I can wait to see if anyone shows up.

In strolls the man bun. He has a nice, sleek fitted suit on today, but he still wears it casually. His beard is well-groomed but long. A few inches in length. No tie. The top button of the undershirt, undone. The suit blazer is dark with some subtle vertical grey stripes. I feel like he could wear it to work, a wedding, or the bar all exactly the same. He just has style. His man bun is very clean too. Sides freshly shaved. Everything else just trimmed. Hairline, strong. The bun itself isn't too big, just enough to be noticeable and form a bun. He is carrying a giant Brown Bean cup.

> **Kevin:** Good to see you!

We share a smile.

> **Kevin:** How's life? What are you doing here?

Someone: It's actually been great. Thanks for everything. I somehow managed a first block spare.

Kevin: Lucky you. Come in and sit down. We can catch up for a bit. I don't have much going on yet. Usually takes a few weeks for the storm to start.

He leads me into the office that looks unused. We sit, and in a rare turn of events, I start the conversation because I have a burning question.

Someone: What's in the cup?

I think I know the answer, but I want to hear it. My narcissistic ego requires it.

Kevin: Just a little blonde roast.

He gives me a subtle nod. Yup…I knew it.

Kevin: Anxiety?

Someone: The hallways and new people. They are a confusing, spinning mess. I just don't know.

Kevin: Well, you got here, to me, so you are doing something right.

Someone: I guess. How did the triathlon go?

Kevin: Not great. I finished seventh.

Someone: Oh. Wow.

Kevin: It's super competitive. Some of the athletes don't have other jobs. They do it full-time. I just can't compete with someone working out fifty hours per week, but winning is just a cherry on top. I got a cool vacation. I kept my mind busy. I spent time with my wife. Winning would have just been something to bring home and brag about to the teachers around here.

He cracks a huge smile.

Kevin: Anyway, there is a lesson here.

His face turns serious.

Kevin: Failure isn't the end. It's the beginning. See the next morning, I woke up and I was still the same person I was the day before. Now I have a clean slate though. I can re-evaluate why I failed. Over the next few days, you reflect, find the flaws, then you correct.

He stands and looks out the window. I can tell he is still reflecting, trying to reconcile what his next move will be.

Kevin: Anyways. What about you? Tell me about your last month or so.

Someone: Everyone at the pizza shop is cool. Dad is happy that I am settling in.

Caleb, one of the employees, took me under his wing around here. His friends are cool. We're getting along.

Kevin: What about on the course side?

Someone: I got a good balance. Things that transfer over to writing well. I heard Ms. B is pretty tough.

Kevin: You're not the first to say that. I don't talk to her much, but my guess is that most students are looking for the easy route and she wants to challenge them. How about the anxiety?

Someone: It's been good and I am running, but I don't know if I am doing well.

Kevin: Use yourself to measure. Keep competing with your last run. If you constantly improve, you are doing well. It takes a good three or four months to build up the running muscles. Keep at it. And writing?

Someone: I haven't been writing much. Figured with school there would be lots of writing.

Kevin: Don't confuse writing for school with writing for yourself. They are completely different.

I give him a puzzled look.

Kevin: You see, school work is assigned. You probably won't get opportunities to go outside the lines or speak your mind too much. School writing is a skill, but it isn't the same. It will teach you how to write to provide. What I am talking about is writing from the soul. No rules. Whatever the mind and body want to write. There isn't an outline. There isn't a deadline. It's just you.

Someone: What should I do then?

Kevin: I think you should start a journal.

Someone: You already said that. Isn't that a little girl thing?

He snickers a bit.

Kevin: Well, I would say journals are popular with little girls, but writing doesn't belong to anyone. Don't think of it as a journal then. Write a few paragraphs every night before you go to bed. Whatever is on your mind. Summarize your day. Call out something that frustrates you. It will clear your mind. I bet you anything you will sleep better. Just do it on your phone.

Someone: I'll give it a shot.

Ms. B

SEVEN cats. That's how many I think Ms. B has. She hands out a syllabus and says she runs senior English classes like college classes. She gives you the tools and feedback, but you have to want it. I don't know what a syllabus is. After some quick research, I discover every other teacher hands out something similar but refers to it as an outline or course description. Ms. B must feel hers is superior and needs a superior name. The list of assignments is intimidating. Three novels. Five papers. Poetry. Shakespeare. The novels are independent study. There is a list of approximately fifty books, and we are responsible for picking three.

At this moment, something occurs to me. I have barely read any books. How can I write a book if I don't read books? I am always a little late to the party, but too impatient to wait. I read the last *Lord of the Rings* book before the movie came out. I read the last three *Harry Potter* books because I couldn't wait for the movie. At my previous schools, they made everyone read the same book. I remember *To Kill a Mockingbird*. The rest bored me to death.

Ms. B also has an entire page devoted to her rules. Here are a few that stand out:

All assignments should have proper spelling and grammar, even if not expressly stated.

All assignments must be double-spaced, computer typed, Times New Roman, with 12-point font.

No talking.

No passing notes.

No phones.

No phones.

No phones.

No plagiarism.

No ghostwriting.

She forgot a few though:

No fun.

No high marks.

Keep creativity to a minimum.

No phones.

Some teachers have inspiring quotes and posters in their rooms. Not Ms. B. She has one poster up. It is of a cat hanging. You have probably seen it around. It was popular in the eighties. All it does is further support speculation as to how many cats she has.

How can I describe Ms. B as a person? Imagine if your mom was actually your grandma. Some teachers push sixty; she might be older. She dresses and carries herself as though she belongs in a retirement home. It is strange that somehow she skipped straight to bitter grandma. Today, she is wearing big square oversized glasses. Her hair, grey and frayed. The sweater she has on was either knit herself or purchased from a thrift store. Purchased probably isn't the right word. The thrift store would have given it to her at the counter because it had been sitting on their rack for over a year. It is that trendy. This isn't a huge leap, but I am guessing she probably doesn't own a cellphone, and the technology she keeps around her house is on par with a crank phone, tube TV, record player, and VCR. A relic of the past. Clinging to existence. The world passes her by, and she fails to evolve. It is actually kind of sad.

All that said, I am still excited to try my best. I want to keep writing, and this is my gateway to college. Plus, the class has a few people I know already. Fast talker from homeroom. Caleb, eating an Oh Henry! in the middle of class. Most notably, though, is Samantha.

These last few days have been so fast that I haven't thought about Samantha much, but seeing her in this

English class brings back that anxious feeling I had before.

Caleb warned me Samantha was pretty popular, and sure enough, she is firmly entrenched with all the cool kids. I have already gravitated towards the outcasts, so it isn't all that surprising she hasn't gone out of her way to acknowledge me. In fact, I don't think she notices me in class. The way she smiles. The way she talks. Something about her is so natural and raw that it doesn't really matter where she is or what she is doing. She just always draws my attention. She has on the Studio Ghibli shirt I bought her. A nice subtle nod, even if she isn't thinking about me. She is talking to a person that looks familiar.

Tall. Lengthy. Lean. Probably has a six-pack. Perfect eyebrows and eyes. Brown hair coming to a subtle slight spike down the middle with a little extra length in the front. Trendy clothes. Probably four hundred dollars. This guy isn't my favourite and I know what it is that irks me. His laugh. Fake, excessive and long. It screams frat boy.

This is the third time I have noticed him. I bumped into him in the hallway on the first day. Then, shortly after that, I saw an ad on one of the million screens plastered around the school. The ad caught my eye because the school has a long-distance running team, and I was considering it. This guy in class talking to Samantha, he was the same guy from the ad.

Business Essentials

BUSINESS Essentials has a special teacher from a local college. When I got my courses, I was relieved to see this was indeed on my schedule. It happens to be my last class of the day on the first day of class. The classes rotate, so it will also be my first class tomorrow. When I arrive, there is a slide up on the screen. It is pretty generic and reads, "*What is Business?*"

No teacher shows up. Ten to fifteen minutes pass. We are chatting. Confused. Most of the students are on their phones. The slide changes. "*Are you staying focused? Discussing amongst yourselves what is business?*"

Ten more minutes go by before, finally, a teacher walks in. She looks young and in good shape. Probably close to forty, but could pass as around thirty. She wears a sharp-shouldered blazer. Her hair is blonde and tied up with a bit hanging down around the sides behind her ears. Her voice is deep and firm.

Teacher: Alright. Any volunteers? Come on. You had twenty-five minutes. What did you talk about?

From the back of the room, a student speaks up. It's one of the popular girls I haven't talked to.

Student: I think business is what our parents do.

Teacher: True. But can you do business?

Student: Ummm...I guess so.

Teacher: Of course you can. Good...good. Anyone else?

Student 2: I think business is making money.

Teacher: Oh, yes. Most certainly an aspect.

Student 3: I think business is following rules.

Student 4: It has to be fair.

Teacher: Good...Good. Yes. Yes.

Student 5: Business is hard.

Teacher: Undoubtedly.

There are a few seconds of silence.

Teacher: Business is filling a need. Business is organized. Business can be anything.

Another pause as she scans the room.

Teacher: At a micro-level, is there a Domino's Pizza around here? What about a Starbucks? Those are filling a need. If there were no coffee shops, someone would see it as an opportunity, then open their own. If they didn't open a Starbucks, another person may eventually come along and open one, once the price is right. It costs money to license the Starbucks brand, but if the community is supporting a local coffee shop, perhaps there is enough demand for a larger chain. Can you be the person that sees the void and fills it?

A bunch of wide-eyed students stare back.

Teacher: At a macro-level, business is so much more. Starbucks started with an idea: we want to bring coffee to market. Then that idea expanded. The right people were brought in. They stayed on top of the trends. They branded themselves and found a way to stand out. They treated employees fairly. They created something so much bigger than a local coffee shop, they were forced to expand because the market demanded it. Or did they expand and then force the market to demand it? That's the razor's edge of business, knowing when you have the power. Some businesses are trying to solve really big problems or bring really big ideas to market. Places like Google and Facebook are reinventing the world we know, and they do it as businesses. I am Ms. Cooper. This year, you will learn about businesses.

She then walks out. A few minutes later the last slide comes up. It is a task. "*One paragraph. You have 30 minutes to write a pitch. I want 30 pitches tomorrow. No bad ideas. Go!*"

That was it. The students look around at each other. This is different than every class ever. At night, I think about what would make a business. What can I bring to this world? Am I a writer? Am I a runner? Am I a student?

I am excited to get to school. I arrive ten minutes early and wait. Ms. Cooper shows up right on time. No attendance. She just starts talking.

> **Ms. Cooper:** Part of business is communication, so I am going to start with an open call. Anyone want to share?

> **Student:** I actually kind of have a business. My dad owns a family restaurant, and I think he wants me to take it over.

> **Ms. Cooper:** Yes, the family business. Very common. Some businesses are passed from generation to generation, providing along the way. Then they find the right mix of people

and take off, or they don't. Those people move on.

Student 2: I want to grow, uhhhhhhhh...tomatoes?

Ms. Cooper: Interesting. You have to be careful when growing "tomatoes". Lots of red tape.

Ms. Cooper throws up two fingers on each hand as air quotes as she utters tomatoes.

Ms. Cooper: Businesses can be illegal. They come with danger. If you are not careful and do something the wrong way, you risk punishment. At the same time, there is always a path. Things that are viewed as illegal, or taboo, can often be tremendous opportunities for entrepreneurs. Anyone else?

I get nervous. Anxious. I want to share my idea, but can I? Do I have enough strength to conquer my fear of failure? My fear of speaking? I let go.

Someone: I want to write a book?

Ms. Cooper: Yes. Yes. About what?

Relief cascades over me, then fear again.

Someone: I don't know. I guess about the things I like?

Ms. Cooper: You see, what is often not understood is that art can be business. You will have this amazing creative journey to make this piece of art. Your book. Then you will have this second amazing journey, turning your art into a business. What I love about art, you set the price. You set the rules. It can be anything and at the same time, it can be a business. Business is a form of art in itself. If you can master the skills of business, planning, marketing, finance, compliance, growth, management, then you are potentially creating a masterpiece.

A pause.

Ms. Cooper: Three fantastic ideas. I am going to number you off. I want you to discuss all your other business ideas, and we are going to start a group project to create a business plan.

I have anxiety. I want to work with Caleb, but it's out of my control. Fear so strong, my heart races. Hoping I get grouped with him. The next three minutes are excruciating. She notices people are sitting with friends, and she starts grouping people that are sitting closest to the ideas as if those ideas are radiating out from an epicentre.

Ms. Cooper: Anyone want to change groups? Raise your hand.

A few students do. One from my group pipes up.

Student 3: I want to work on the tomatoes.

Ms. Cooper: Okay. Fair enough. Follow your passion. Everyone, follow your passion!

A few students move around. The groups are not even. It doesn't bother her. She hands out a document. It has some very basic business questions.

Describe your business:

Who is your customer?

What is the need this business fills?

How do you deliver your product to them?

What are the obstacles?

Ms. Cooper: As a group, discuss all your business ideas first. You don't have to go with the original idea. If you have a different idea, discuss it.

We ravage away for ten minutes.

Ms. Cooper: Okay, and time. Did anyone change ideas?

No one speaks up.

Ms. Cooper: Does anyone want to change?

One of the people from the family business group raises their hand.

Ms. Cooper: Yes?

Student 4: I want to make a video game.

Ms. Cooper: Oh, my. Great, great. I love all the ideas.

She stops for a few seconds of pondering.

Ms. Cooper: Okay. New fourth group. Video game. Come over here. Anyone.

Some quick discussion among the groups. Five additional students go over.

Ms. Cooper: Okay. No one is committed to anything yet. Discuss as a group how to achieve your ideas. If you come up with a different idea, you can present tomorrow.

The groups gather in tighter. I start the conversation for my group.

Someone: How can we all write?

Caleb: We don't have to all write. I can be the manager. Help you organize, make connections, and sell the book.

Someone: Cool.

Someone's Story

Mystery Girl: I am good at English.

She wears glasses, but they are not off-putting. They fit her well. Long brown hair that is straight to her shoulders. Her eyes are blue behind the glasses. She has a nerdy vibe. Great posture. Well put together.

> **Someone:** You want to be the person that fixes my bad words?
>
> **Mystery Girl:** Like an editor?
>
> **Someone:** I don't know what an editor does.
>
> **Mystery Girl:** By the way, it's Erica. My uncle is an editor. He reads other people's writing and fixes the spelling and grammar. Sometimes though, people also ask him to help write. To help improve the characters and the plot. He says editors are the technical flow of creative energy.
>
> **Someone:** Sweet.

There are still two more people. Caleb looks over at them and then munches on a sandwich. I have no idea where he got it or when he pulled it out. These two have already digressed to reading posts on their phones.

> **Caleb:** I think I know what else we need.
>
> **Someone:** What?
>
> **Caleb:** Marketing.

Erica: For sure. My uncle says he has read lots of good books that didn't get marketed well and never sold. That part is hard. You can make something amazing and then fail to get it out to the world.

Caleb: Okay. Let's make marketing a two-person job, and marketing can help everyone else.

Someone: Agreed. Wow, we have a team.

Now all I have to do is just write a book.

Coffee

SCHOOL is going great. My classes aren't proving too difficult. Once you get used to the building, it isn't that hard to get around. Caleb and his friends are awesome. Caleb was slowly giving me a social media tutorial. I never used it before, and after a couple of days at school, I was already feeling the pressure. Everyone is on it, but I am still on the fence. The first thing Caleb does is show me memes. He talks about all the summer trends. Bed Intruder, Inception, Vuvuzelas. I love Vuvuzelas. They are so annoying, but in a charming way. I am starting to see the appeal a little. Some of this stuff is funny. Going viral is a term I have only heard in regards to the cold where I was from.

Work is down to one or two shifts a week, just enough to pay my own way with the car and have a little leftover for fun.

I have a new habit too. It isn't a diary. Nope. Every night around nine, I pull out my phone and write whatever is on my mind. Just a mind dump. Clear out all the garbage. What I find is I am sleeping great. Apparently, I haven't had a good night's sleep in years, because once I started doing my brain dumps, I can relax by ten and go to bed, free.

There are two things I am struggling with. Dad and Samantha. Samantha is distant. We never get one-on-one time at work anymore. She hangs around a totally different group at school. In fact, we haven't talked much at all since I found out about Josh. If anything, Josh has made me shyer and more reclusive. I am not looking to challenge anyone. I am not one to take charge. When I see a stubborn Type A person, I just stay away. There is no point in challenging them. They think they are right. I can't win. Just move on and pick my battles. Josh is not a battle worth fighting. He is unpredictable. A variable I can't control. He could potentially attack if threatened, and I want no part of that.

I feel bad about Dad. I want to spend more time with him. I am still cooking a few nights per week and giving him every Sunday to do whatever. He is really looking forward to a new show called *The Walking Dead* on AMC. AMC had a breakout hit with *Breaking Bad*. Amazing show that Dad and I always watched together. Deep down, I think a piece of him wishes he could have been a meth cook. It would have been such a thrilling life. Luckily for us, we got to instead watch it unfold on TV as a fantasy.

I am hoping *The Walking Dead* will be good, just because it is my "Dad Time" and we lost *Lost* from our TV schedule when it wrapped. The premier date is Halloween, but we would PVR and watch it whenever. I don't know much about the show. It is based on a comic and is AMC's next big push. Small cable channels are showing some very interesting programming. They were not being as restrained by advertising standards, they can go a little further. Making the experience almost like an extended movie.

The big networks, ABC, NBC, Fox, are vanilla. Afraid to take a risk. AMC, Showtime, and HBO are willing to go the extra mile. They show movie theatre quality gore, have a little bit of questionable language and nudity. These are off-limit at the big networks, but have been going into films for years. The smaller cable channels jumped on the opportunity to bring adult themes to the TV screen on a more drawn out schedule. Ten-hour seasons as opposed to two-hour movies. It works if the content is good. You are happy to spend an extra eight hours with Walter White every year.

My big score this month is convincing Caleb's crew to come for coffee. They aren't big coffee drinkers. I am looking to change that, and I figure getting them outside of school might get some better conversation than the usual lunchroom yelling match due to the general noise level. I don't know them that well at this point, but I want to. We agree to Monday after school. I will drive. I have also planted the blonde roast seed.

Brown Bean is never empty, but also never busy. Today is no exception. The perfect balance. You need other customers to pay the bills, but too many customers and it loses the appeal. Everyone is wearing hoodies and jeans. The unofficial school uniform.

Someone: So, who drank their dark roast coffee?

Caleb: It tasted like tar.

The others nod.

Someone: Yup. That was the point.

Geoffrey: Can we just get hot chocolate?

Someone: Give me one chance.

I go up to the till and grab four blonde roasts then take them to my corner. Caleb and Geoffrey look at me kind of weird. I am not sure why. Four people, four coffees.

Someone: Okay, let me walk you through this. Pick up the cup and smell the roast. It almost has a nutty aroma.

Geoffrey: I don't smell it.

Caleb: Did you really try?

Geoffrey: How do you not try to smell?

Caleb: It's a metaphor.

Geoffrey: "It's a metaphor."

Someone: Give it a little swirl just to wake it up.

Geoffrey: I don't think mine is sleeping.

Caleb gives him a playful punch.

> **Someone:** Now, take it and slowly put it to your lips. You barely want to get any. It might be hot. You just want to get a tiny taste and swish it around on your tongue. Go on. I will walk you through it.

They all proceed to follow my steps. Ashley and I make extended eye contact, like she is asking me something. I let her know she can trust me. This will be good. I promise.

> **Someone:** The first thing you will taste is pretty much the same as any coffee. Let it sit around just a touch. Now swish it. Did you taste it? You should have found something nutty, soft, almost with a hint of cocoa.

Caleb swallows.

> **Caleb:** I taste it. That's amazing.

> **Ashley:** I taste it too!

We all smile.

> **Caleb:** Is there food in this place? I am hungry.

He flags down a barista, and before we know it, a plate of donuts is in front of him.

Someone: What's the deal with school?

Geoffrey: I am just tired of that place. There are so many meathead guys and airhead girls. Chasing likes and living inside their phones. It makes me sick. Sometimes I just want to stand in the hallway and scream at the top of my lungs. They don't know what real life looks like.

Ashley: We all feel like that.

Caleb: That's why we are friends.

Geoffrey: We are more like people who tolerate each other because of mutual hatred of the masses. Introverts that get each other, but live on the fringe.

We all smile a bit and hit the coffee again. We talk another fifteen minutes. Caleb and Geoffrey have to go. I hang around a bit longer with Ashley. She always talks more when it is just the two of us. After a while, I mention Erica is putting something together for Halloween and she could come. I had already invited Geoffrey and Caleb anyways. I don't really know what we are doing. It is sort of a hangout, but also maybe about our project. It isn't a Halloween party, it is just on Halloween. Erica also happens to be born on October 31, but when she told me, she was clear this wasn't a birthday party either. I honestly don't know what it is supposed to be, but I want to go.

My Ears

LOOKING deep into my locker, and minding my own business.

Locker Girl: DID YOU HEAR THE NEW KATY PERRY ALBUM IT'S SO GOOD I COULDN'T BELIEVE HOW MANY OF THE SONGS WERE GOOD IT WAS LIKE EVERY SINGLE SONG WAS A HIT SHE IS AMAZING I WISH I COULD BE KATY PERRY HER HAIR IS AWESOME AND SHE IS SO RICH IF I WAS RICH I WOULD TRAVEL SO MUCH TRAVELLING IS FUN I TRAVELLED MOST OF THE SUMMER WITH MY PARENTS AND THE HIGHLIGHT WAS DISNEYLAND DID I TELL YOU ABOUT DISNEYLAND ALREADY OH WELL I AM GOING TO TELL YOU AGAIN DISNEYLAND WAS AWESOME I LOVE DISNEY I HAVE SEEN ALL THE CLASSICS SNOW WHITE BEAUTY AND THE BEAST THE LITTLE MERMAID BUT LIKE THE NEW ONES TOO TOY STORY IS AMAZING I HAVE

WATCHED ALL THE TOY STORY
MOVIES LIKE FIVE TIMES EACH EVEN
THE ONE THAT JUST CAME OUT ALL
THE PIXAR DISNEY MOVIES ARE
GOOD MY LEAST FAVORITE IS CARS I
ONLY SAW CARS ONCE DID YOU SEE
CARS DID YOU LIKE IT I THINK THEY
MADE THAT ONE MORE FOR BOYS SO
YOU PROBABLY LIKED IT
DISNEYLAND WAS AMAZING IT HAD
EVERYTHING I ALSO SAW TWILIGHT
I LOVE TWILIGHT EVERYONE DOES
THE FIRST ONE WAS SO GOOD NOW
THEY ARE GETTING CRAZY DO YOU
PLAY ANGRY BIRDS I LOVE ANGRY
BIRDS ANGRY BIRDS IS THE BEST
BECAUSE YOU CAN PLAY IT FOR
JUST A FEW MINUTES OR YOU CAN
PLAY IT FOR LIKE AN HOUR THE
GRAPHICS ARE SO CUTE SOME OF
THE LEVELS ARE SO HARD YOU TRY
LIKE SEVEN TIMES AND YOU CAN'T
BEAT IT THEN SOMETIMES YOU BEAT
A LEVEL ON THE FIRST TRY WHEN I
AM NOT ON ANGRY BIRDS I AM ON
FACEBOOK DO YOU HAVE
FACEBOOK EVERYONE DOES YOU
CAN POST THINGS LIKE HOW MUCH
YOU LOVE ANGRY BIRDS AND THEN
YOUR FRIENDS ARE LIKE OMG I AM
PLAYING ANGRY BIRDS TOO AND
YOU CAN SHARE PHOTOS OF YOU
PLAYING ANGRY BIRDS BETWEEN
FACEBOOK AND ANGRY BIRDS I
BARELY PAY ATTENTION IN CLASS

Someone's Story

SPEAKING OF CLASS I THINK THE
BELL IS GOING TO GO SOON.

This is not the first or the last time I shut my locker
door with my head spinning.

Chances

OUT of the blue comes a choice opportunity for me. Closing the store on school nights was not allowed. My dad makes school come first. My phone rings. It is Bambino's. Samantha is on the other end.

Samantha: Are you busy!

Someone: Was that a question?

Samantha: Are you busy?

Someone: Nope.

Samantha: Just what I wanted to hear. The other driver had car trouble and can't come in. I know you said no school night closing, but we need you!

I want it. Not for the money. For some time with Samantha. To be the hero and save the day.

Someone: Hold on. I'll call you back in a few.

I beg my dad. Homework is done. First lie. It isn't. I need the money. Second lie. I want to work with Samantha. After five minutes of begging like a dog for a treat, he agrees to let me do it just this time. Back to the phone. It rings twice and then Samantha answers.

Samantha: Bambino's Authentic Italian Pizza, Samantha speaking.

Someone: It's me. I'm in.

Samantha: Oh, good. Hurry over. Toni is driving for now, but he has to go. It's crazy.

I fly over. The first few hours of the shift are the typical high-octane, pressure-packed, adrenaline-charged, pizza delivery dinner rush I have become accustomed to. It eventually slows down, as the rush always does. Now I get some time with Samantha.

Samantha: Hey, thanks for saving us tonight.

Someone: It's all good. I just had to convince my dad. He is a school first guy.

Samantha: Sometimes I wish my mom cared more about us. She's always gone.

Someone: How is school going? Senior year!

Samantha: I know, right? I just want it to be over. It's not really my thing.

Someone: You are so popular. You must like it.

Samantha: I don't like keeping up with everyone. It's too much work. You're in my English class, right?

I know she is, but I play stupid, like I don't spend a few minutes each class glancing over at her.

Samantha: I hate Ms. B. She is such a B.

I laugh. First time I have heard that. Anyone who goes to the school probably has heard that a dozen times, but the joke works on me, and the fact it works on me gets a rise out of her.

Someone: Who are those guys you hang around with?

Samantha: It's all the athletes. They're cool. Kind of typical jocks. They like to party, and I like free parties. I know a few of them from all the way back in elementary school.

Someone: I didn't take you as a girl who hangs with jocks. If you had asked me last month to describe your friends, I would have said trench coats and cigarettes behind the school.

Samantha: Because I look like a goth, I must be goth? Looks can be deceiving. Goth is in. Everyone does it. Crazy hair colours and cool tattoos. They were talking about banning certain hair colours last year because so many girls were doing it, but in the end the fad kind of died down. I still love having my red streaks.

Someone: Those red streaks are sweet.

Samantha: Thanks.

Someone: Caleb said something happened with Josh?

Samantha: I don't really want to talk about it. He is all kinds of drama. Worse than my girlfriends...

Someone: Come on, get specific.

Samantha: You sure?

Someone: Educate me on some big city drama.

She chuckles.

Samantha: Okay...where to start...let's start with the little things...so he doesn't think things through or ask for my opinion when he makes decisions. It's soooo frustrating. Like for dinner the other night, I went to his place around seven. He ate by

94

himself at six and didn't leave anything for me. Frustrating and ignorant. Then the other night, he wants to go into the city to take some photos because he is a hobby photographer on the side. Well, it's kind of fun to pick out locations and stage the camera, so I say yes. We get in the car, and like three minutes in he points out that he needs gas and he has no money. I am like, really? W-T-F? Maybe you should think about that before you propose going into the city. Of course, I pay for it, but again, he is just ignorant and frustrating.

She pauses to catch her breath.

Samantha: You ready for the big oh shit moment though?

Someone: Hit me.

Samantha: He has a kid.

I already knew, or at least speculated as such, because Caleb had brought it up. I pretend not to know.

Someone: What?

Samantha: He has a kid. Like for reals. And he didn't tell me. There is this other girl from a few years ago, and he described it as a party where everyone was a little overly drunk. End result. He has a kid. They're not a couple, and they never really were.

Someone: So what does that mean for him?

Samantha: Child support for eighteen years.

Someone: No shit, eh.

Samantha: Ya. It was kind of my get out moment. So back to single life.

Someone: It ain't so bad.

She smiles.

We wrap up the rest of the shift. I do the dishes and drive her home. I feel like I rescued the shift, and now I have an opportunity.

Back to Business

A few classes come and go. We learn all kinds of business concepts. Opportunity cost was one of my favourites. You have two decisions. Each has a cost. Some costs are intangible, and you define their value. If you want to go to a concert, the ticket might sell for fifty dollars, but you wouldn't give that ticket up for five hundred dollars. But what if your dad were sick? Would you skip the concert to be with him? That is opportunity cost. Trying to find the value of things by comparing them.

At the same time, this skill involves some economics and accounting. It all comes together and forms daily business decision making. We also learned about human resources, conflict management, job design, recruitment, and retention. After that, marketing. How to sell a product and hit an audience. How to make something viral. Eventually, we get to finance. The bean counters and red tape. Compliance, control, safety and security. Currency is interesting. Fiat is when a currency is no longer backed by a tangible material and instead backed by the government, which can issue it infinitely by raising their national debt. It is kind of scary. The government can print a billion dollars tomorrow and devalue every dollar already in existence.

The video game group, they can't decide what game to make because two people want creative control. Our group? We don't have an idea for what we are going to write yet, but Erica and I are going to lead the charge, so to speak.

During the video game debate, we cover problem-solving. The teacher tells us this is one of the most powerful business tools. Effective problem solving defines a business. Our current problem, one group wants to make a game like C.O.D.; the other wants to make a game for phones. The teacher lets both sides present a case. Then, in a moment of clarity, she decides, why don't you instead make a game development company? You can make both games and share resources.

My mind is set on fire. It is as if the answer was there all along, and we didn't have the ability to see it, but she did. She then comes to each group and offers some coaching. How to make our projects work. Some of the obstacles we might see.

For us, she says making art is very much an individual process and it can take immense amounts of time. You may not finish your task for years. In fact, churning out a finished book at this stage would almost be a miracle, but the roles are unique enough that she thinks we can proceed and we will have a solid business plan at the very least.

The only pain point right now is our two additional group members aren't doing much. I caught them drawing giant veiny male private parts on the debate assignment. Then I tapped Caleb and asked what is going on here. He bursts out laughing and gives me homework.

That night, after my dad goes to bed, I watch *Superbad*. Comedies are not something I watch much of because my dad isn't into laughing much. *Superbad* is epic and I understand why Caleb was laughing in class because I hold back my laughs in the middle of the night.

The Party

EIGHT weeks into the school year and most of my weekends have been me delivering pizza. I like the rush and the social side of the job. On this particular Sunday night, I am free of that obligation. Instead, my attention is on an invite from Erica to hang at her place. A Halloween and birthday party with nothing to do with Halloween or birthdays. My dad took a little convincing as it is a Sunday night, but Monday is a day off anyway. I told him we would be at Caleb's. What he doesn't know is we aren't at Caleb's. We are at Erica's. Her mom is divorced, and Erica convinces her into date nights every now and again when she wants the house to herself. She has an older brother. She says that he is a big stoner, and he moved out two years ago to go to college. He left most of his stuff behind, but it is cool stuff. I am really excited because Geoffrey, Caleb, and Ashley are also coming.

I drive up around eight. It is a townhouse complex. The night makes it hard for my eyes to distinguish the finish. Parking is scarce, but I weave my way through until I find an opening. Then make my way to the door and I ring the bell. Nothing. I ring the bell again.

Maybe I have the wrong place? Maybe they were trolling me...

> **Ashley:** Sup.

Ashley's standard greeting. She has one bud hanging down and the other in her ear. Once inside I am impressed. The hallways are well-finished with white moulding, top and bottom. The floors are dark hardwood. Everything is bright, and there is plenty of light reflecting off the white walls.

> **Someone:** Not much. Who else is here? What's the plan?
>
> **Ashley:** That's a surprise.
>
> **Someone:** Where is Erica? This is her place, right?
>
> **Ashley:** She is busy, but I can show you around.

Ashley gives me a quick tour of the main floor. The place is bigger than you might think. Three bedrooms. Two bathrooms. Clean. We end the tour, heading downstairs to the basement. It's not what I expect at all.

The walls appear to be painted black, but it is hard to distinguish because there is almost no light. Most of the visibility comes from two black lights nestled on opposite ends of the room where the ceiling meets the walls. The second source of light is the fish tank. Large and glorious. The darkness of the room makes the glass and water disappear. The little fish castle radiates a colourful glow accompanied by the many neon silicone shrubs. A few fish weave in and out, also catching the purple light.

The last source of light. It is the source to behold. To the naked eye, on a regular day, you can't make out the tones of Ashley's hair, but in this room, that one tone of white has turned to four different shades of green, all of them glowing under the black light. My eyes can't look away. I had no idea you could even make your hair glow.

Ashley makes her way to the couch and forces her way between Caleb and Geoffrey. Caleb occasionally stuffs cheese puffs into his mouth. They are both fixated on the TV screen. Much to my joy, they are playing Super Nintendo. Vintage gaming, black lights, Ashley's hair. This night is going to be a blast.

The game of choice is *Super Mario Kart*. A classic. Strangely, Erica is nowhere to be found. In the background, there are at least four tower speakers, maybe more are hidden in the darkness. The playlist is an eclectic mix. Bouncing between Eminem, Kanye West, and various indie-rock tracks I had never heard.

After about ten minutes of getting loose and everyone getting a turn, the real game starts. Erica comes in and pulls out four shot glasses, all glowing neon. I think they call it radioactive glass. She positions two each near the controllers and pours something from a jug. Then she pulls out the vodka and tops off each.

The usually soft-spoken and brief Erica then opens up with what almost seems like a pre-rehearsed speech.

> **Erica:** The name of the game tonight is Drunk Driving. The rules: One-on-one...Winner advances...You must down your first shot before you start driving...Your last shot is reserved for when you cross the finish line...Round one is all on the same track...Round two and round three are on random maps...The loser is always eliminated...Oh ya, new rule tonight...If you don't have a controller...

She pauses and pulls out three more glasses.

> **Erica:** You still drink.

The next two hours are a furious flurry of shots, yelling, and bonding. If I had to guess what was in the jug, grape Kool-Aid? But I am not 100% sure. This might have been the best night of my life up until that point. I can't remember who won. Somewhere around the fifth shot, it starts to get blurry. We didn't talk about the project for a second, or at least, I don't remember talking about it. We did talk about how it felt good to not be trick or treating like the children. Like we were finally growing up a little.

I don't make it home.

When I wake up, there are a few seconds of confusion, trying to remember the last thought. We were playing Mario Kart. I was not doing well. Then I just remember trying to find the floor.

Erica is already up. The others are gone.

> **Erica:** Hey, man. You went hard.

> **Someone:** It's not that. I just rarely go, so even one or two shots is hard. You guys don't party like they do in the small towns.

She laughs.

> **Erica:** Well, everyone had fun. I hope you guys will do this again. Maybe next time we'll actually get the project started.

> **Someone:** I am down for anything, anytime. Just send the invite.

> **Erica:** Slow down. You need to walk before you can run.

> **Someone:** Happy birthday.

> **Erica:** You didn't have to say that. It's okay. Every day can be a celebration. It doesn't need to be a birthday to be special. You hungry?

> **Someone:** Yes.

> **Erica:** Come with me.

She takes me to the kitchen and gives me a big bowl of Cinnamon Toast Crunch with a small glass of orange juice. It tastes amazing.

Failed English Assignment

MONDAY was a write-off. I was hungover most of the day and didn't want to face my dad. I tried jogging to burn most of the morning. It sort of worked as a hangover cure and absolutely worked as an avoidance plan.

Tuesday morning. *The Great Gatsby*. I am sure it is a fine book. I didn't read it though. Between jogging, working, my budding social circle, and keeping up with my dad, something had to give. Never one to read, it was an easy decision as to what to forego. I have done this before with other novels throughout the years; *The Outsiders*, *Alice in Wonderland*, usually resulting in a B or a C. This time, my plan fails as Ms. B and her cats see right through me. Getting a bad mark isn't the end of the road, but it is a blow to my ego.

Straight to the library with laser focus. I find a nice quiet booth off to the side and dig around my bag until I manage to find *1984*. This is not a book I am unfamiliar with. Although never having read it, many of the movies I like cite *1984* as an inspiration. I get through a few chapters.

Across the library, I see a face I recognize. He is deep into his phone with a giant smile. I walk by once to try to get a closer look. I think he was messaging a person named David. I know exactly who this person sitting here is. His name is Trevor. He is the guy I don't like who frequently talks with Samantha in our English class.

One of my other observations, every time he looks at his work, he is frustrated. Every time he looks at his phone and sends something to David, he is happy, even giving his annoying frat boy chuckles now and then. I make my way over.

Someone: What class is that?

Trevor: Ms. Bitch gave me a D on my report. I have to keep a C average to keep playing sports.

In addition to being the running team captain, Trevor is the star wide receiver on the football team, and that is just what I know so far. He probably plays all the sports. He isn't getting an education in academics. Nope. He is getting an education in sports. To each his own.

Someone: Can I see your report?

He reaches down and hands it over. The page is littered with red circles. He has no grasp on paragraph structure, struggles with the use of there, their, and they're, never uses too, always just to. It is like a scene in a horror film. My first thought, if this is a D, how is mine an F. My spelling and grammar are way above this. My finish and structure rival anyone else's in the room. On that alone, I should have managed to beat this D.

The second thought. I spend the rest of my spare giving Trevor some one-on-one training on the basics of the English language. He doesn't pick up any of it. Not really a surprise though. Grade four is about where I would put his education level. This is when I begin my negotiations.

> **Someone:** I have a deal for you.

> **Trevor:** Okay?

He looks at me like a child confused by the principle of negotiating.

> **Someone:** What if I wrote your next book report? What would you do for me?

> **Trevor:** I could pay you.

> **Someone:** I don't want money.

> **Trevor:** I could...

Typical Trevor. He needs to be spoon-fed.

> **Someone:** You could let me be on the running team.

> **Trevor:** I could let you be on the running team?

Someone: You're the captain. You must be able to make it happen.

Trevor: It isn't that simple. Coach gets the final call.

Someone: He must listen to you though. Can you make it happen?

Trevor: I will try.

Someone: If you get me on the team, I will guarantee you a B on your next assignment.

Trevor: Guarantee?

Someone: Guarantee.

Trevor: Get me a B and I will do whatever you want.

We leave it like that as the bell rings for the next block. My plan is to read *1984* and write two papers. One will be for him. I will add in some of the errors I saw on his paper. Use the wrong word here and there, but cut the errors in half and make sure the analysis is stronger. I don't need an A, just a B. I feel like if I can write one A paper, how hard can it be to change that to two B papers?

A few days later and Trevor gives me the news.

Trevor: You're in. One of my guys got hurt and can't go this time. We run in January.

Start training. Get under five and we'll see about future events.

Grad Fundraiser

EXTRACURRICULARS and me don't mix. I don't play sports. I was never on the chess team, the debate team, or in the drama club. Even if they had a film club, I wouldn't have gone. Just not my thing.

Sadly, during grad year, there are some obligations that require me to put in school time outside of school hours. This does not thrill me.

Frankly, I don't even know all the events that are planned, but what I do know is that I am the treasurer for the bake sale. See, I don't bake. My dad doesn't bake. The other two options besides being involved in the bake sale were to wash cars, more reserved for the cheerleaders, or pay your way. There are better things for me to do with my money than pay my way. Hence, we find me running the till at a bake sale.

It isn't just once. There are three weekends scattered throughout the year and a talent show. We do it Friday AM with the morning drop-off, and then we also have a booth at the local farmers' market Saturday morning. Friday AM is pretty popular. We set up right at the front of the school and catch all the students coming in, as well as the parents heading out for work. Lots of parents are buying huge quantities. My guess is they are buttering up their office colleagues with the assorted sweets.

Running the bake sale till is nothing compared to a Bambino's dinner rush. The bake sale is busy, but not hornet's nest busy. It is a breeze. Early on, I see Geoffrey and I take the opportunity to ask him a burning question.

Someone: Hey, man.

He doesn't notice me at first behind the counter.

Someone: Geoffrey?

His head pops up.

Geoffrey: Oh, hey!

He lights up with a smile.

Someone: What are you looking at?

Geoffrey: Didn't eat breakfast.

Someone: We got some cool muffins.

Geoffrey: Oh, shit. Gimme.

I hand him a Nutella-stuffed chocolate muffin.

Someone: Keep it quiet, but this one is on the house.

I smile, and he nods back.

Someone: I got a quick question though.

Geoffrey: Oh, the price of the muffin just went up?

Someone: Sure...an answer for a muffin. So, Caleb and Samantha. What is the deal there?

His face changes a little. The smile is gone, and he looks more serious.

Geoffrey: They are complicated. We are all complicated. There are things about us you just don't know yet because you have only been here a few months. Give it time. One day Caleb will tell you. We all have our secrets.

I know he is hiding something about Caleb, Samantha, and himself, but I also understand I have to earn it with trust. He leaves and I pull some personal money out to pay for his muffin.

What I didn't know going into the event was that Locker Girl was organizing grad. There was a brief break in the action, and she took the opportunity to talk my ear off, as was normal.

Locker Girl: AREN'T YOU EXCITED FOR THE DANCE OR IS IT THE

CAMPING TRIP OR THE TALENT
SHOW WHICH EVENT ARE YOU MORE
INTO CAMPING IS ONE NIGHT RIGHT
AT THE END OF THE YEAR WE ARE
DOING HIKING SWIMMING A HUGE
S'MORE CAMPFIRE THEN AN
ASTRONOMER-LED STAR VIEWING
PARTY I CAN'T WAIT IT'S GOING TO
BE AWESOME EVERYBODY IS GOING
TO FREAK OUT WHEN WE FINALLY
GET THERE!!!

She went on for another couple of minutes. At least I
now have an understanding of what the grad events
are…

Harry Potter

THE pace of this year is unrelenting. Blackout, move, counselling, jogging, job, new friends, new school, class projects, grad planning. It just never lets up. On a plus, time is flying. We are months into the school year, and something has kind of snuck up on me.

You see, I come from the generation that grew up on a common story. We were all in grade school when the first one came out. At first, only the bookworms were in on it, then the nerdy kids, then the nerdy adults, then the movie buffs, and within a few years, everyone.

I am talking about *Harry Potter*. It reintroduced reading to my generation. These were the first non-school novels that I have strong memories about. I remember standing in line to get the Order of the Phoenix and reading it cover to cover in a weekend. Daniel Radcliffe, Rupert Grint, and Emma Watson were actors, but we spent ten years watching them grow up with us. From wide-eyed children to awkward teens, and finally, early adulthood. It mirrored all our lives. Even though it was fantasy, it felt real because they had our problems.

Why am I bringing all this up? *Harry Potter and the Deathly Hallows: Part 1* just came out. The studio wanted to do the last book "justice", and so they decided to make it two movies to keep as much of the story as they could and get the extra box office revenue on their golden goose.

This is a must-watch. Everyone is going to see it on opening weekend. I am going with Caleb and his group. Erica has been joining us more and more. After her amazing Mario Kart night, we have basically accepted her into our circle.

The theatre is only a five-minute drive from school. We all cut class to catch the afternoon showing. I am not big on cutting class. My dad has zero tolerance for that. This is a cultural event though, so I agree. Caleb picked up the tickets weeks ago.

A quick introduction to driver licensing. They have a three-stage program. L. You can only drive if your L is displayed and you have a fully licensed driver in your passenger seat. N. You must display your N. You can drive alone. Zero tolerance on intoxicated use. You can't have more than one passenger if no one in the car has their full license. Then, of course, full license.

I am in the N stage. We pack the five of us into the car, and I just pull the N off. If you're going to break one rule, you might as well break two. I drive like a saint to avoid any "heat". They laugh at me for adhering to the rules of the road a bit more than usual, but I don't want to give the cops a reason to pull me over, as I could probably get my license suspended and I need it for work. Also, five minutes.

The theatre isn't empty, which I thought it might be seeing how it was the afternoon. Nope, probably eighty percent full. That's how big of a draw this movie has. Try going to the dinner show. I am sure it will be at capacity.

Caleb and I have read the books. Geoffrey kind of knows what happens already, but never read the books. Ashley never reads and has kind of grown out of the phase, but feels obligated to see it through. Erica, I don't know.

Ashley sits next to me during the movie. A few times I feel like she looks over and maybe puts her hand on me on purpose. It is dark. We are all sort of touching. I can't tell if it was an accidental touch.

We are walking back to the car after the movie. Caleb is eating some of my left-over popcorn. Ashley has already popped in an earbud.

> **Caleb:** What did everyone think?

> **Geoffrey:** Is it me or does Hermione keep getting hotter?

> **Caleb:** It's funny seeing how dorky Rupert Grint turned out and how hot Emma Watson became. She is like a solid nine, which is not

really the book character but whatever. He is like a four.

Geoffrey: I thought more people were going to die.

Ashley: Ya. Killing Dobby was sad and all, but not much happened. It was kind of slow

Caleb: I thought it was slow.

Erica: So slow. Like nothing was really happening most of the movie. They're just stuck in a tent, crying.

Someone: I was a little skeptical going in. My concern was this was going to feel like half a movie. There isn't a true payoff. Nothing really happens with Harry. They're in the same place as when the movie starts with a little more knowledge.

Caleb: It's hard having to wait to see it end. I do think they did the book justice. By doing two movies they kept pretty much everything.

Geoffrey: We have to wait until July? The movie is probably done already. They're just holding onto it to make more money.

Someone: For sure. Are any of us not going to go? I know I would pay anything to see how this ends. They could charge fifty a ticket.

Caleb: I would pay fifty to watch it.

Geoffrey: Totes.

Erica: Well, duh.

Ashley: Yup.

We gather into the car.

Erica: Hey, guys. One more thing.

We all look at Erica.

Erica: The last week before Winter Break, I was thinking…

Someone: Yes.

Caleb: Hell yes!

She doesn't have to finish. We all know. We keep talking our way through the ride home. I am giving them door-to-door service, one by one. I like to observe houses. It's a window into a person's day-to-day lives. How neat is the yard? How big is the garage? Is there even a garage? How many windows?

First off is Geoffrey's. It is nicer than I expected. The yard is perfectly kept. Double lot, for sure. Double car attached garage. Looks like a dozen visible windows. Geoffrey probably has it pretty good.

Someone's Story

I already know about Caleb's trailer from talking, but I have never seen it. Always dropping Samantha off at the gate to the park. It is funny because I have two different versions. One is the Samantha version. Total dump. Falling apart. Drafty. The other is the Caleb version. He says it is small but does the job. When we arrive, I lean more towards the Samantha version. Broken concrete on the driveway. No garage. A couple of shingles teetering on falling from the peak above the front entrance. It is run down. I am guessing based on what I have gathered about the family situation, they probably rent. Something is better than nothing.

Next is Erica's. I have already been here. The only part I dislike is navigating the maze to find her townhouse again.

As for Ashley, we make our way to the coffee shop instead, where she finally takes her bud out. I am pretty exhausted from dealing with all the social obligations, but I always say yes because I know what life is like to have none.

Ashley the Enigma. Friends are hard. Ashley is always gone. She is always quiet. I think she is a friend. We hang out. She acknowledges my existence. That is better than ninety-nine percent of the school. So yes, we are friends.

Someone: You seem distant.

Ashley: Sorry.

Someone: What's up?

Ashley: I don't know. I am just done with the kid stuff. It doesn't do it for me anymore.

Someone: You didn't have to come.

Ashley: The weird thing is, I wanted to come. Then, while I was watching, I was bored.

Someone: Well, that sucks.

Ashley: I do enjoy hanging with all of you though. I hate school. I hate my mom. But I like you guys.

Someone: Here is an interesting fact.

Ashley: What?

Someone: I have known you for months, but I don't know where you live.

She gives a huge smile.

Ashley: I'll keep it that way.

Someone: You sure?

Ashley: Positive.

What is this girl hiding? She doesn't like being questioned. It's part of her vanishing act.

Someone: Look, if you don't want to talk, you don't have to. I have been talking. With the counsellor, Kevin. It helps.

She looks puzzled.

Ashley: I didn't peg you as the counselling type.

Someone: It's a long story.

Ashley: Go on.

Someone: If I share, you share.

Ashley: Hmmm...maybe the whole story isn't fair. Let's start small. I have one big question. Something I can't peg about you.

Someone: I am intrigued.

Ashley: Girls.

Someone: What about them?

Ashley: You are not like the others. What is it? Are you gay?

Someone: Wouldn't say that.

Ashley: Why are you so easy to talk to?

Someone: I am looking for similar souls. Guy, girl, why does it matter? I want a mental connection first.

Ashley: So do you like me?

Someone: I don't know you.

Ashley: Yes, you do.

Someone: No, I don't.

Ashley: I talk to you as much as I talk to anyone.

Someone: But what are you talking about?

She pauses and sips.

Ashley: Then who?

Another deflection. She is good at that.

Someone: That isn't an easy question. It's going to be a long time. It has to be a strong bond. I don't know what they will look like, but there are some key features I am looking for.

Ashley: Like what?

Someone: They talk. They aren't afraid to express things deep inside. They are fun. Time goes faster when I am around them.

123

Someone's Story

Ashley: You mean like right now.

Someone: Exactly, but not just once. It has to happen over and over again.

Ashley: Well is there one?

Someone: Maybe.

Ashley: Who?

Someone: I don't know.

Ashley: Come on.

I ponder, but I think I trust her.

Someone: Samantha.

Ashley: Really...why? You don't talk.

Someone: Not anymore...I worked with her over the summer.

Ashley: What happened?

Someone: It was confusing. I liked her, but I never said anything. She moves so quick with guys. I just didn't want to ruin what I had with her. Now it is slipping.

Ashley: Does Caleb know?

Someone: I think so.

Ashley: Huhhhh...

She is perplexed.

> **Someone:** At any rate, that's a bit about me that is new. Tell me something about you I don't know.

She chugs back her coffee.

> **Ashley:** Not yet.

> **Someone:** That's not fair.

> **Ashley:** Life's not fair. You'll have to do better to earn my secrets...

She gives an ear-to-ear grin. I hate her right now, but I like the tease, and I think she knows it.

Determination: Dig Deep

THE weather is frightfully cold. A man with an eighty-eight on his chest is sitting on a rock. He looks exhausted. His balaclava has been heaved onto the ground next to him. Steam radiates from his hair, which is all over the place. His shadow has grown in. It has been days since he shaved. On the ground are his socks. They are red from blood.

The runner is examining his foot. He has it pulled up as close to his face as he can get it. There is a quarter-sized blister on the back where the shoe meets his heel. A toenail is teetering awfully close to falling off, badly chipped and bleeding. He doesn't want to touch it. It's that fragile. Another blister near the landing spot at the front. Beyond that, there is just a general fatigue, wear and tear. These feet have been busy over the last few days.

Due to the temperature, these toes can't stay exposed for long. He is trying to wrap some gauze around the worst of the wounds. He digs in his bag, trying to find fresh socks but can't. Instead, he reaches down and grabs the bloody socks. Slowly, he pulls them back onto his feet. There is pain in his eyes. It takes minutes to get the socks back on. He needs a break before he can continue to his shoes.

He goes for his water. It's bone dry. Then he pulls the map out. He looks around. There are no flags to mark the path. There are barely any footsteps to follow. He is fingering his way around the map, trying to figure out where he is. How much further to the next checkpoint. He needs warmth. He needs socks. It looks like he is only halfway. There is still a long journey ahead.

For a few seconds, a thought creeps in. He could pull out his GPS and end it. He could hit that button, and they would come to find him within an hour. That's the easy way out. While looking down, a tattoo slips out from under his sleeve. Not Done.

Every failure from his life cascades into his mind. The jobs he quit. The people he left behind. The people who left him behind. It's real pain. Blisters might hurt, but they always heal. The pain he is feeling right now is the kind that is so deeply rooted, it is attached to his central nervous system. He is shaking violently, curled up in a ball, like an addict going through detox. This is the kind of pain thinking of quitting brings to him. His body outright rejects the thought and forces him into convulsions until he can clear his mind.

He stands. Rolls up his sleeve. He doesn't care that it is freezing. He cracks his neck left and then right. Stretches out his arms. Puts wet shoes over bloody socks. Pulls on the frozen balaclava. Puts two fingers to his heart and raises them up. Then he starts running. One foot after the other.

Just another day at the office.

The Real Party

IT is about a week before winter break. A couple of months have passed since the Mario Kart night. We all wanted to get together again, but between work and school, we just couldn't find the time. Having to wait for another group night added to the anticipation.

Ashley is shrouded in mystery. I have known her for close to three months now, but she only shows up to school seemingly every second day, and when she does show up, she barely speaks. The amazing thing is she isn't getting kicked out, so she must be crushing the tests. If she valued attendance and participation, she could be a straight-A student with a scholarship to wherever she wanted. But that isn't her. She doesn't care about what others think of her. She just does what she wants. She is near impossible to track down outside school. I'm not a nosy person, and Ashley has deflected the few times I have asked her almost anything personal.

It's around eight, Erica's orders. I let myself in and head down to the basement. Same people as last time. The black lights aren't on. I can see everything now.

There are four smaller speakers around the room. The
fish tank looks kind of sad in regular light. The
conversation is on what music we will be listening to
first. They are at an impasse and need me to break the
tie.

Caleb has scored an early leak of Kanye West's *My
Beautiful Dark Twisted Fantasy* from Pirate Bay and
already listened to it, saying it was perfect. Ashley
wants to listen to her custom mix that she describes
as depressing indie folk-rock. Erica wants to listen to
techno. Geoffrey likes all music. It came to me to
break the tie. Kanye West isn't my favourite, but I
didn't mind *808s & Heartbreak* and my gut is telling
me to go with Kanye.

> **Someone:** If I am breaking the tie, I go with
> Caleb and Kanye.

I get a few dirty looks.

> **Erica:** Fine.

> **Someone:** So what are we playing tonight?

> **Erica:** Oh, we aren't playing anything.

I am a little confused. I was ready for some gaming
again. What the hell is she up to now? She turns off
the lights, leaves the room, and comes back in a white
cloak with the hood up. She is so theatrical. The
black lights kicked on. Ashley's hair lit up. Erica
reaches under the table and pulls out two bags of
gummy candy. There aren't that many though. I could
polish off a good fifty by myself, and one bag has

five, the other, twenty or so. Everyone else is fixated on the gummies as if they were made of gold. My confusion is visible. She hands everyone one of the gummies from the bag with just five. They all pop them fast and look at me in anticipation. I know something is up. Maybe these are joke candies that taste funny. Or maybe mine is a laxative. They snicker and smile while I eat it.

It doesn't taste like a gummy, it is barely sweet, and a strange aftertaste lingers that I can't place. Wouldn't call that candy. Hopefully, it isn't a laxative. For the next thirty minutes or so we just talk until everyone gets up and sits around the coffee table.

Erica picks up her gummies again and starts walking around the circle. Her hand goes into the bag almost in slow motion, like it is a ritual. She doesn't just drop them on the table. She treats the bears like they are more than just candy, setting them down directly in front of each person. She is meticulous in ensuring the bears appear to be holding hands, all facing the same direction, feet towards us. There is a level of mysticism and spiritualism in the room. Everyone gets three or four more bears, but when Erica comes to me, she pauses a little longer. I only get one. A wise decision from our shaman. Seemingly, only I am in the dark as to what is coming next.

She sits down and gets into the lotus position, her eyes closed. I had no idea she did yoga. Everyone else is in some makeshift sitting position. I keep my eyes open though. After a minute holding the pose, she reaches down and picks up the stereo remote. She holds it for another few seconds before pressing play, all the while, eyes closed.

The bass drones away. An angelic voice comes on. It repeats a few times. It's almost like the music tells them when to eat the first bears because at the moment the beat changes, they all slowly ingest, eyes still closed.

The unmistakable voice of Kanye West comes on. I pick up my bear and examine it. Spin it along my fingers, pondering what kind of cult I have gotten myself into. Give it a sniff. I only eat half at first. Nothing special. It's time to join them, so I shut my eyes and try to get lost in the music. When the second angelic chorus comes on, I eat the other half, keeping my eyes shut. The song continues. At the end of the track, I peek around to see what is going on. They are all still sitting. Fairly motionless and eyes closed still, so I close mine again.

The trademark out-of-tune Kanye beat comes on. Another good song. The third track is *Power*. His big summer single. Everyone has heard it a dozen times by now, but it doesn't feel out of place or overly familiar. A sign that Kanye knows how to put together a full album that flows. Around this time is when the edibles kick in. I open my eyes. The posters on the wall are starting to melt. Ashley's fiery green hair is hypnotic. Erica's cloak glows more than ever. I get lost for a few songs, watching the fish weave in and out of their neon decorations. I am dizzy, but not sick. I just want to not move.

The song is *Runaway*. The simple yet mesmerizing
piano intro. I am staring at a one-inch guppy that is
changing between neon green and light purple. It
weaves in and out of the various pink structures and
fake dark purple seaweed. The fish are slowing down.
I can hear their gills. Every little movement of the fin
is met with great expectations. Then, all of a sudden,
the fish makes a quick break for the pink castle. It
scares me back to reality. I have been gone for fifteen
minutes. Once I come back. I pull out my phone and
just start taking notes. After writing for a bit, Ashley
comes over.

Ashley: What you doing?

I don't answer.

Ashley: You've been writing for forty-five
minutes.

I still don't answer.

Ashley: Have you ever been high before?

Someone: Not like this.

She looks over. Erica is still sitting in lotus, gone
from the world.

Ashley: Erica goes deep.

Someone: No shit.

Ashley: I like it. Come on. What are you
writing about?

Someone: Us. Moving here. The people I've met. This.

Ashley: Me?

Someone: Yes.

Ashley: What about me?

Someone: That you are mysterious.

Ashley: You think I am mysterious?

Someone: I know you are mysterious. It's not a thought. We have sort of known each other for three months, and I know almost nothing about you except that you keep your buds in.

Ashley: What do you want to know?

Someone: Just talk about yourself.

Ashley: I don't do that.

Someone: Not only do you not talk about yourself, this isn't the first time I have tried. You are always gone too. Hence, you are mysterious.

She laughs.

Ashley: What specifically?

134

Someone: Talk about your family.

Ashley: Fine…broken home. Mom has a good job. She makes too much money. I am an only kid, and I get spoiled rotten. Whatever I want and basically no rules.

Someone: The buds?

Ashley: What?

Someone: What is the deal with the buds?

Ashley: I do that to escape reality. Numb the surroundings. Tolerate the world.

Someone: What about me?

Ashley: I like you, but we are friends. I don't want to complicate the group. We have a good thing going. I try to keep my dating game to people outside of school. That place is a social disaster without mixing love into the equation. Besides, I know you are chasing Samantha.

Someone: Keep that quiet! It's a secret!

Ashley: Sorry.

I actually kind of agree with her though. These are the best friends I have ever had. It's one of the reasons I have been careful around Samantha. I need to make sure Caleb is okay with it. So even though I do like Ashley, I love our little ragtag team more. I just always wonder what's going on behind the eyes. Now I know a little more.

Unnoticed by me, Erica has left her lotus and is behind us. She raises her arms up to ensure she has our attention, her cloak glowing under the black lights.

> **Erica:** I heard you mumbling. I have an observation.

> **Someone:** Was I mumbling?

> **Erica:** You were definitely mumbling. My observation. Whatever you are putting in that phone right now. That's your book.

She is right. The notes I have been keeping the last few months, as well as my recent flurry of writing tonight. This is the start of something. I tell my pizza stories. We talk about family, friends, and fun. The next few hours are a mind-boggling brainstorming session of everything that has happened to us in the last few years, with me front and centre. I leave out a lot about Samantha. I'm sure they kept their secrets too. I feel amazing. I reach for my pocket. My keys are gone. I start to panic.

> **Erica:** Your keys are hidden.

What?

> **Someone:** Where?

> **Erica:** You are not driving.

Someone: I am fine.

Erica: No, you are not.

Someone: I am.

She gives me a look I have never seen from her before. I know I can't win this. I guess I am going to have to sleep it off. I don't put up a fight and I write a little while longer, then crash hard.

The next morning, I wake up and I barely remember anything. I find the note in my phone and am amazed by how much I have written. Erica has Cinnamon Toast Crunch for me and fills me in on the evening. I don't know what to think. My head is spinning a bit.

When I leave there is a present in my shoe. The note doesn't say who it is from. I think it is Ashley. She had said she was going away for a few weeks when we were talking earlier. The note just says to open when I am bored. I keep looking over at the present the whole drive home.

Talent Show

I am standing at my locker gathering for the day.

> **Locker Girl:** AREN'T YOU EXCITED
> FOR TONIGHT IT'S THE TALENT
> SHOW WE PUT IN SO MUCH WORK I
> CAN'T BELIEVE IT'S FINALLY
> HAPPENING WHAT ARE YOU DOING?

Another of my duties for grad is to help run the till
for the door and food during the talent show. I sort of
get to watch the show for free too. I am about to say
something, but it's near impossible to get a word in
with this one.

> **Locker Girl:** I HOPE IT ALL GOES
> WELL AND LOTS OF PEOPLE SHOW
> UP THIS IS GOING TO BE AMAZING
> EVERYONE IS GOING TO BE
> SOOOOOOO GOOD ARE YOU IN THE
> SHOW?

I don't answer, but my thought is hey, running the till
is a talent. Just a talent no one is going to cheer for.

Locker Girl: THAT'S RIGHT YOU ARE THE TREASURER SORRY OF COURSE YOU WILL BE THERE THEN OH MY GOD OH MY GOD OH MY GOD!

The day ticks away until eventually, dinner rolls around. Our gate opens at five. I have another guy with me, but I don't know him at all. I stick him on the door. Figure it won't be too hard as it's the same price for everyone. That is a bit of an optimistic assumption, and somehow, within a few minutes, the door is short thirty dollars. He might have taken it. Whatever.

The theatre looks like it belongs to the multiplex downtown. It is amazing. A beautiful red curtain. Fifty or so rows of padded, stadium-style, premium seats. A full-on snack bar with a nice metal roll-up window at the back of the room. This is where I am. Above me is another room where the controls are. This theatre has it all. Spotlights, projectors, surround sound. The drama teacher and some of the students are running the control room.

I am slinging popcorn, soda, and hot dogs for forty-five minutes solid. Then the line starts to die down to just the occasional person that is probably trying to skip the rush of earlier. Soon, the event gets underway. Most of the acts are fairly underdeveloped. Like you would expect. Anyone going to the school could perform. It's a school-wide talent show presented by the grads, so it isn't just our grads performing. We are facilitating.

A student I don't know does some bad ventriloquism. Another does standup. A teacher does some slam poetry. There is a group of girls that sing "Barbie Girl" by Aqua. This is one of the highlights for sure, and a real contender for audience favourite. Then something none of us are ready for happens.

The lights dim. A single spotlight on the stage. It's one person and an acoustic guitar. I recognize him instantly. It's Geoffrey. He never mentioned he was performing. I have no idea if he is any good. He strums the guitar. Just the strum sounds beautiful. The guitar is perfectly tuned. Until now, his eyes have been on the ground. Ten seconds have passed, where he just lets the strum reverberate around the room. He looks up and blasts a confident E minor out of the guitar. His voice sounds like he is whispering to us after eating sand and smoking cigarettes. Another E minor strums, and he lowers his voice.

At this point, he has the audience absolutely captivated. He continues the opening verse with his low, grizzly acoustic tune.

He transitions to a C and starts the chorus. It's a slightly higher key. He doesn't lose the grit, just opens a little further. Holds a few notes a little longer. It's like a muscle car going forty. You know it's capable of so much more. You can hear the restraint.

The last D rings out on the guitar. His eyes have drifted down again. He holds for a few seconds, letting the D fade. The next sentence is a return to the grizzled, sandy whisper from the start. A few people in the room haven't placed the song yet, but all are in awe. He blasts a huge powerful E minor, picks up the pace, and lets go of a perfect "Whoah", much louder than anything he has caressed us with so far, almost like a sudden ear assault.

Geoffrey is singing *Livin' on a Prayer*. It's not the rock version though. It's a moody folk cover and it is really good.

A few minutes go by and then he finishes to thunderous applause. He isn't done though. The cover is just a warm-up. Now for the main event. He lets the noise level off. A few moody strums.

Geoffrey (singing):

When the lights go out and the noises fade away

It's clear to see how much has changed

The happy life we led is oh, so far away

And this room feels like a cage

Watching you was profoundly hard to do

Its harder still to go alone

I can't forget all the worries we went through

Every word weighs heavy like a stone

That intro was haunting. It is almost too much to take in, but then his chorus sends chills around the room.

Geoffrey (singing)

Let me go, it hurts so much

Let me go, I've had enough

Let me go, if I could only forget your touch

Maybe I would hurt no more

Maybe I could live again

The room is mesmerized. This isn't some high school student singing; this is a manifestation of greatness. Deep emotion combined with rare talent. You can feel pain. I had no idea Geoffrey had this in him. Remarkable and inspiring. I will never look at him the same again.

Fire Jog

BOOSTED by Geoffrey's rousing acoustic performance, I feel the urge to do something more. Something special. I have to be capable of finding another level. The talent I just bore witness to is so awe-inducing it leaves me with a desire to improve. To try and achieve the perfection witnessed. There is some healthy jealousy. My outlet is jogging.

Today, my beat of choice is Eminem. During the summer, *Love the Way You Lie* was inescapable and a return to icon status for Eminem. That song tells a story in five minutes. How could you not love it? The real jogger's tune is *No Love* though. It has high beats per minute, and when Em drops his verse, the tempo is unreal. If this song doesn't pump you up, check your pulse. Once I am warmed up, I find *No Love*. When the venom starts flowing, it has an immediate effect on my blood flow. They may just be words, but they accelerate my blood just like a snake bite would. With each step, my pace quickens. All-out sprint.

It's amazing what a song can do. It's amazing what an inspiring friend can do. When I check my tracker,

I am running a sub-five. Flying! I am going to crush this team event.

Geoffrey's Home

THE next day, Caleb, Ashley, and I are all settled in for lunch. I know who I want to talk to though. Sure enough, he comes in. To everyone else he is different. He doesn't care. In his mind, he is still the same person. The room actually gets silent for a half-second. People take notice of him as he walks over to our table.

Geoffrey: Today's been weird.

Caleb: How?

Geoffrey: Everyone is treating me different.

Someone: You realize you are different.

Geoffrey: Am I?

I stop and try to imagine being him for a second. What could it possibly have been like to have had a secret like that? He had been holding it in because I think he was afraid everyone would look at him differently. He did something that he loved, and he just happened to do it in front of people. Our

145

perspective of him is shattered, but he thinks everything is the same.

> **Caleb:** You know what you did.

> **Someone:** Come on, man, you can't expect us to just ignore that.

> **Geoffrey:** You don't have to ignore it, but don't think of me differently. I am the same.

> **Caleb:** Are you still you?

> **Geoffrey:** What do you mean?

> **Caleb:** The old you would have never played in front of the school.

> **Geoffrey:** I guess so.

> **Caleb:** Hence, you are different. You did something different. You showed a different side of yourself.

> **Geoffrey:** In my head, I was building up to this. It just felt like the natural thing to do. Hence, I feel exactly the same. Just like natural old me. Lots of practice. Nights.

> **Someone:** You are weird.

> **Geoffrey:** Thanks! I needed that.

He gives a giant smirk.

Someone: I feel like I barely know you. Like how? When?

Geoffrey: We do barely know each other. You are a new friend. Caleb is an old friend. He knows things about me you just don't know because of time.

Someone: Like what?

I look over at Caleb. Caleb looks over at Geoffrey as if to ask permission. Geoffrey nods back.

Caleb: I knew he could play. I knew he was good.

Someone: You never said anything.

Caleb: I feel a person has to be ready to share. I don't want to put extra pressure on them. When they're ready, they're ready. Plus, there is something driving him you don't know.

Someone: How do you know?

Caleb: I have been to his house.

Caleb and Geoffrey lock eyes again. Geoffrey nods, but this isn't the same nod. Caleb's expression goes dark.

Caleb: He has a wall of music. Posters and records. It is his passion, but he was afraid to fail. Stage fright, if you will.

147

Geoffrey: Yup. Hated the hour before. It was like someone took their hands and squeezed the air from my lungs, then held them crunched up in a ball.

That's dark.

Someone: How did you get through it? The fright.

Geoffrey: Mom.

Caleb and Geoffrey share a glance again.

Caleb: I think he is ready.

Geoffrey isn't very emotional in general. I see some rare emotion.

Caleb: Geoffrey?

Caleb reaches over and hugs him. I am confused. Clearly, they know something I don't. Geoffrey fights off the tears and manages to fight out some words.

Geoffrey: Today...

A long pause.

Geoffrey: After class...

Someone: I don't know what you are talking about, but anything you need.

Caleb: Just come with us.

Something very emotional is waiting for us. I spend the next few hours wondering about it. Geoffrey never talked about his mom. Caleb brought it up. Everything changed. What is wrong?

As soon as class ends, I race to my locker and then my car. Sure enough, Caleb and Geoffrey are waiting.

Geoffrey: Are you sure?

Someone: Anything, man.

Caleb: He is good.

Geoffrey: All right. Let's do this.

We don't talk much. There is a heaviness in the air. It feels like my old house. I have already been to Geoffrey's house once, but just to drop him off out front. This time, we park and make our way in. Geoffrey quickly shuttles us around back to a rear entrance into the basement. Apparently, this is a thing. Most of the kids my age seem to have the basement. A little place to call their own. It is very organized. Bright. Light grey paint with white trim. Unlike other basements, this one gets plenty of light. It has lots of windows. Isn't submerged under the earth. There is a full bathroom, a bedroom, and a living area. It has a small kitchen too.

Someone: Wow. Is it just you?

Geoffrey: It is.

Someone: This is cool.

Geoffrey: I guess. It's nice and all.

Someone: What do you mean? You basically have your own mini condo.

Geoffrey: If that's what you want out of life.

A deep, puzzling answer.

Geoffrey: Come here and look at this.

He brings us over to the couch. There is a fifty-inch TV and 5.1 surround sound. The wall is decorated with platinum albums and music memorabilia. Next to the TV, an electric guitar sits, perched on a stand with pride. An acoustic guitar rests to the right, both gorgeously maintained and pristinely displayed. The wall art is Nirvana, Green Day, and Hendrix. This guy loves music so much, but almost never talks about it.

Someone: Why don't you talk about music more?

Geoffrey: Music is my everything. What if I am not good enough? What if I can't make it? I am afraid to bring it up because I don't want to fail myself. This is my shot.

Caleb: Dude. Come. On.

Someone: Ya, man. You are no failure.

Geoffrey: Do you know real failure? To try so hard at something, but not achieve it. To get close, but then fail. Do you know how much that hurts? To not be able to achieve what you wanted. To fail yourself. To fail those around you. To feel alone. To find yourself curled up in a ball crying. Have you ever felt that? Nights. Entire nights. Over and over again. It actually hurts to play, but that is where the power comes from.

Wow. I knew this guy went to dark places. We share a moment, looking at his wall of music.

Someone: What is the failure? The thing that gets you to play all night.

Geoffrey: It's not my failure. It's my dad's. The doctor who tried to fix something and failed. He got so lost on the journey, he was never the same.

Someone: What did he try to fix?

Geoffrey: Why we came.

Someone: I thought we came for that.

Geoffrey: No. That's my escape.

Oh my. Where is he going with this? He shuttles us back outside and around to the front again.

Someone: You have a separate entrance?

151

Geoffrey: Completely. My family is complicated.

He knocks. A small woman in light blue scrubs with ice cream cones on them comes to the door.

Geoffrey: Hi Maria. Can I see Mom?

Maria: Of course. She is resting, but you are always welcome.

She welcomes us inside and offers drinks. The main floor has a similar finish. Light grey with white trim. Lots of light. There are six diplomas up on the wall. Geoffrey has smart parents obviously. We start down a hall. Geoffrey stops us.

Geoffrey: Okay. You think you know me, but you don't. You are about to see something, but it will all make sense in a few minutes. I don't like to talk about it. It's better to show.

I nod. This is a different Geoffrey. Open, vulnerable. His shell, removed. We make our way into a room. There is a woman laying on a bed. Geoffrey reaches in and gives her a giant hug. Not much of a response. It takes me about a quarter-second to put it together. That is Geoffrey's mom. Geoffrey has tears coming down his face.

Geoffrey: Hi, Mom. I have a new friend. This person is really cool.

I step over. He grabs my hand and pulls it to hers.

Geoffrey: Mom…

He can't finish his sentence. I am starting to well up with tears now. Geoffrey caresses his mom's hand, which is now sitting on top of mine. Then, I feel it. Geoffrey feels it too. A slight squeeze back. We both just hold her for minutes. Caleb watches from the door, also getting emotional. He has clearly done this before, and he is giving us our moment. Eventually, Geoffrey wipes back the tears.

Geoffrey: It's MS. Not much longer left.

Someone: I'm so sorry.

Geoffrey: Hey, I know you don't even have a mom. I got a good decade. That's better than some.

This is so sad. You shouldn't have to only get a decade with your mom. It does get easier, but I never really had a mom so it wasn't hard for me. This looks so painful.

Someone: And your dad?

Geoffrey: He is a doctor. He tried to help. He was trying to treat it. He couldn't. It broke him. Now he is never around.

I give him a big hug. He slowly makes his way out of the room and leads us back to the car.

Geoffrey: Now you know. Music is my escape. I play for her. All night, sometimes. It's not some ego thing. Don't ever confuse my music as being some ego thing. I am too young to feel this old.

I hug him one more time and then make my way to the car with Caleb. Once we are alone, I turn to him.

Someone: Dude.

Caleb: Dude.

I don't know what to say.

Caleb: That guy is dark. His life is dark. It's pure pain, every day. Whenever you think you have it bad, turn and look at that guy. He has been living like this for years. Every day he goes to school and puts on the smile for everyone else, but there are heavy clouds over him.

Someone: Holy shit. I don't even think I can drive right now.

I am shaking. I am spinning a bit. My anxiety problems seem so insignificant. I am having a panic attack for Geoffrey.

Caleb: Let me drive you home.

Someone: You can't drive.

The words shake out from me.

154

Caleb: I have my L. You're the one who can't drive now. It's only a few blocks.

Caleb gets me home. Somewhere along the way, he pulls out Skittles. This time, he shares. I don't have words. I don't know what to say or do. I am just trying to hold it together and eat Skittles.

Caleb: Give that man his space. Let him have his time with his mom. He will figure it out. Look what he just did. Be there when he needs you, but not more than that. I just want to help him. That's all I can do. Always help him. Laugh at his jokes. Answer his calls. Anything he needs.

I nod.

Someone: How are you getting home?

Caleb: I'll walk. I could use some air anyways.

I understand.

Someone: Thanks for letting me in.

Never judge a book by its cover.

Winter Break

O N the last day before break, I manage to find
Kevin. Geoffrey's situation is bothering me. I
had misread it. What can I do?

Someone: I am noticing a trend.

Kevin: Go on.

Someone: Most of my friends, they have
weird houses?

Kevin: Like they are crooked? Or old? Or
broken?

Someone: No. No. No. Umm...I had a friend
who has a nice house. I had a perception of
him because of it. I was wrong. His house
was...I can't find the word besides weird.

Kevin: Do you mean the people?

Someone: Yes!

Kevin: That's not a house. That's a home.

I give a puzzled look.

Kevin: People and memories make a house into a home. Your friends don't have weird houses. They have weird homes. Care to elaborate?

Someone: Well, I don't have a mom. Samantha and Caleb don't have a dad. Geoffrey is basically living alone in the basement and has a family situation. Erica only lives with one parent. Ashley does her own thing.

Kevin: It sounds like you found a group of people with trouble at home.

Someone: I guess. But they are all nice.

Kevin: Don't mistake a home situation as a reflection of the person. In fact, those situations can be very character building. You and your friends are being forced to grow up faster. It's not a bad thing. You are linked by maturity. It's a feeling you all have. Perhaps you are bonding because you are all filling a void home life isn't providing?

He is right.

Someone: What makes a home better?

Kevin: A home should be a special place. It should be healthy and filled with people and things that give you memories. Pets. Photos. Loved ones. That is what makes a house into a home.

Someone: I can't fix that.

Kevin: It's not really your job to provide a home for friends. You can occasionally, but they need to figure out home on their own. Everyone is different. You can show them your home. Maybe they will want that. Talk about it. Perhaps your expectation of a home isn't possible for them. Bad memories, bad people. They have to leave. The halls feel haunted.

Someone: That sounds a bit like our old home.

Kevin: Go on.

Someone: Because of my mom, the air always felt heavy. It's been lighter since we left. It is still just Dad and me, but it feels better now.

Kevin: I think you are coming along nicely. You had a toxic environment, and you left those memories behind you. One of the keys is that once you become an adult, you determine your surroundings. You have the power to change what the walls look like.

> Think carefully about your walls; they are a
> reflection of you.

I ponder all the walls I have seen and who they
belong to. I wonder a bit why my mom left. What
made the walls toxic? I don't think it was me or Dad.
Would I have toxic walls one day? What would I do?
How quick would I notice?

Kevin: Enjoy the break!

Someone: You too!

The mission is simple. Run every day for two weeks.
Read and write every day for two weeks. By the end
of the break, I should have my times under five and
two novel reports written. If only life were so easy.
My mind has exploded in new directions, aided by
the assistance of a few gummy bears, a shaman and a
musician.

No matter what I do, my biggest fan is always Dad.
When I told him I was joining the running team, he
was so excited. We are long past the days of Santa
leaving presents under the tree, so instead, it is Dad
and me at the mall. The goal. Turn my running attire
electric yellow. While there, I notice he is fighting a
cold or something. He doesn't seem sick, but he is
coughing.

An observation. Winter here is different. It's not even
cold. I am used to having the wind bite my cheeks
and two feet of snow. I haven't even seen snow yet,
and the temperature couldn't bite anything if it tried.
It's like a perpetual fall.

New shoes, new headband, new wrist-bands and a new shirt. A living, breathing, running billboard for Mountain Dew! The first run in yellow feels amazing. The air is cold and crisp. The odd gust of light wind. The sky is blue with the odd whimsical cloud scattered. I feel light. The small gusts carry me around like a feather. When I finish, my average is floating around five still.

My first novel doesn't even last three days into the break before it is done. The papers are written by the fifth day. The doctoring down is done by the sixth. Ashley is in Mexico with her mom for three weeks. Her mom, the one she hates, pulled her out of school a few days early to go to Mexico. Poor Ashley. Caleb and Samantha are with their dad. I am not as close with Geoffrey or Erica, so I don't really know what they were up to. I assume Geoffrey is playing guitar for his mom and don't want to bother him. He has my number. If he needs me while Caleb is gone, I will be there in a second.

It is much like when I got here. Just me and Dad. But not everything is good news. Dad had made one stipulation when I took the job at Bambino's. If he said I had to quit, I had to quit. Between the bad assignment and Dad's desire to see me do well in school and running, he lowers the hammer. The job is gone in January. No debate. The decision is final.

I take it with mixed results. Giving up my extra time with Caleb and Samantha will be difficult. Having the extra hundred bucks or so every week has been nice, but I do want to spend some more time with Dad, and I have been so busy we haven't done much of anything together in months. He has been a little distant himself. Although he has never been one to spout his emotions, there is even more of a wall up. Like he is hiding something. It feels like Geoffrey. Over the next week, we get caught up on *The Walking Dead*. Amazing! Then, movie time!

There isn't much debate as to what we will see. *Tron: Legacy*. *Tron* is a classic. A little difficult to watch because of how old it is now. Funny they are trying to reboot the franchise all these years later, but that has become the norm, trying to make a franchise out of something. In the car, I ask him about what my priority should be: school or jogging. He would normally have always said school. This time, he doesn't though. As if he has changed and he has some regret. Instead, he says that athletic achievement is rare and can hold as much value as education. This is unexpected, but I guess what he is getting at is he never achieved anything athletic, so who is he to comment.

As for the movie. The critical consensus is it is a failure because the plot and characters are weak. My argument is you are watching *Tron* wrong then. The core of what makes *Tron* such a treasured cinematic experience is in the stunning, jaw-dropping visuals and over-the-top sound. Seeing the black suits with neon accents. The stark contrast in colour. The visually arresting palette. *Tron* may have a weak story, but it is still worth seeing on the biggest screen you can find. After the movie, I had another treat. Caleb got back from his trip, so we met at Brown Bean.

Caleb: Sometimes I hate my dad.

He stops and takes a bite of his slice of apple pie.

Someone: Hi, Caleb.

Caleb: I don't see him for months, and then the whole time he is just bitching about what I am going to do when I graduate. He is so strict. Controlling. How much do you know about him?

Someone: Not much.

Caleb: You know Geoffrey's past. I think it's time I give you some of mine. Let me tell you a story.

Someone: Go on.

Caleb: When Samantha and I were really little, my dad came home and my mom had bought a bunch of makeup and a purse. He was so angry. He screamed that the money is for the family. He made her eat the makeup, and then he went and burned the purse in the backyard.

My jaw hit the floor. That is insane.

Someone: Caleb...wow...that's....awful...

Caleb: It was pretty traumatizing. I had to sit and watch my mom chew and swallow lipstick with tears rolling down her face.

162

I am not sure what to say.

Caleb: There were years like this. Eventually, my mom got out. We only see him a few times a year. He is way better now, but it is hard to be around him. I still see the old him. I think Samantha was hit even harder. She refuses to talk to me about it. Doesn't acknowledge it happened.

Someone: What does your dad do?

Caleb: He was in the military. Now he works security, but he changes jobs a lot. You know, we are all in these messes. I see it too. You don't have a mom. Samantha and I don't have a dad. Geoffrey has his thing.

Someone: Wow...have you thought about what your dad said? What are you going to do after we are done?

Caleb: I don't know. Probably do nothing. Maybe go travelling for a year. I don't want to just jump at something. There is just so much noise right now.

Someone: Can you afford to travel for a year?

Caleb: I don't spend my work money, plus I could always work odd jobs. It's so cheap in some places that like ten dollars could last a month.

Someone: What about after that?

Caleb: If I had to pick something now, I think I would want to be a pilot, but not a commercial pilot. A cool one.

Someone: Like Top Gun?

Caleb: Exactly. I will be a different person in a year though, so who knows?

We drink to that. It's good to have a friend back. I missed hanging out.

The Box

I still have this mystery gift. It has to be from Ashley. I don't know though. The note on the top reads:

It's a Christmas gift, but it doesn't have to be attached to Christmas. Open it whenever, but save it for when you are bored, alone, and have a few hours to kill.

I am bored, and my dad is at work. I open it. It's a handheld box, maybe five inches tall. I open the lid. There is another box inside. A note sits on top, folded very precisely into a perfect square. I open the note:

Do you trust me? Are you alone for a few hours? Do not proceed until you have a few hours.

I have nothing going on all day. I open the next box. There is another box inside. On top of this one is a sticky note pointing at a pill taped to the top.

Step 1: Take this, then open the next box.

Someone's Story

It's a small, oily-looking pill. I examine it. What could it be? I have my suspicions, but I proceed and swallow. It goes down easy. I open the next box. That's it. Interesting. No next box. There are three notes though. Again, each folded perfectly, and this time they are numbered. I open the first one.

Go for a long jog. Do not open the next note until done.

Weird, but this is fine. I get dressed, and I go for a one-hour run. The whole time I think about the notes back at home and my strange, but awesome friends.

Finally, I arrive home. I am feeling a little off. It's the pill, for sure. My balance feels a little wobbly. I am lightheaded. I get to the box and open the next note:

Go run the bathwater really hot, as hot as you can take, and fill the tub. Take the last note with you and take your phone. Wait another 20 minutes until opening the next note.

I proceed. I can feel the lightness. My mouth is dry. The water touches my skin and feels amazing. Each bead runs off and tickles on the way down. The jogging tingling sensation times a thousand. My eyes are barely staying open. The warm embrace of the water is euphoric on a good day. Today, it feels so good, I can barely stand the sensation. There is a calm to withstanding though. The twenty minutes is a battle. I reach over. My hand moves in slow motion. I feel the water ride down my arm. Every hair is alive. Once I finally get the note open:

166

Put on the album Deep Forest and just drift away.
When you feel right, do whatever you want.

I find *Deep Forest* on YouTube. It is tribal. There
aren't many words. It is primal. This came straight
from the jungle, from nature. My mind races. I can
hear my heartbeat. I drop my head underwater. I can
still hear the music, but now my heart sounds like it is
next to my ear. I think about all the people in my
mind. Their quirks and flaws. Everything about them.
Their bodies. It is so vivid. The beat of music
changing between fast and slow helps to dictate the
mind flow. The hot water ignites my skin. Blissful
euphoria. Eventually, I pick up my phone and start
writing.

Hours go by. I think about Geoffrey, Caleb,
Samantha, Erica, and Ashley. What a life I have
found here, and so quickly. Interesting people. After
some time, a memory of my own comes back. It is
old. Really old. I am in kindergarten maybe. A girl
steals scissors from my table. When the teacher asked
where they went, she points right at me instantly. I
tried to explain what happened, but no one would
listen. Weird memory.

Book Reports

O N the first Monday back, I meet with Trevor again. I give him two doctored assignments. I am happy with the work and proud of how Trevor-like I made the spelling and grammar, but disgusted I had to dive so low.

Over the break, I had managed to polish off three books. This would get me a bit ahead. Trevor's paper compares *1984* to professional sports culture. I figured it was about the only thing he would be able to make an insightful comparison to. His second report is on *Seabiscuit: An American Legend*. Dad has a soft spot for the occasional trip to the pony track, and I was already vaguely familiar with the story, so it was a quick and easy read that I thought might be something believable as a Trevor book.

My reports are pristine. Not a single mistake and a methodical breakdown of the structure. I found the inciting incidents. Identified the motives. Tore apart the obstacles. I made myself into the characters and saw the world the author had built.

Trevor doesn't care what the reports are about, but we do have some common ground, running. I ask him about his typical training. It floors me. No wonder he can't spell. He spends five hours per day working out. It is only after five minutes with him you realize how dense he is. Most girls probably never even make it past five minutes of conversation before they throw themselves at him. That laugh though. It makes me angry. It is fake and cheeky while being arrogant. It's hard to accomplish all those things in a half-second, but Trevor can do it every time he laughs.

We turn in our first report on Monday and have our grades back by Thursday. Ms. B and her cats are quick markers. Trevor gets a C+, which might be his highest grade ever on a paper, but not so high as to raise suspicion. Not the B I was hoping for, but I know I will do better next time. My second report isn't on Seabiscuit. I wanted to make sure we didn't raise too much suspicion. It was extra work for me, but I didn't mind.

Trevor is happy with the results. It is enough to keep him going. He did come through with the running team, and there is just one more thing. I ask him about Samantha. I tell him I worked with her and we had a good summer, but it has been hard to get her to open up. I also tell Trevor I know Samantha hangs around with his group so I was hoping maybe the running team would be my in. His advice is pretty dense. Just ask her. Might work for him, but I don't have his physical blessings. I have to go about it differently. This is not the advice I wanted, but I shouldn't be surprised.

Friday Night Lights

M OST of the school is going. We have our
biggest rival in town. The Bayside Broncos.
Being new to the town, I'm not as invested in
the rivalry, but it has all the hallmarks. We stole their
horse and painted him our team colour. Yes, there
was an electric yellow horse running around town last
year. They painted over our field. We raised our
noses to them because our property assessments were
higher. They won the league championship last year.

I am mildly curious to see how good Trevor is. If I
had to judge based on his writing skills, he must be
amazing. Everyone swoons over him, even the
teachers, so there must be something special I haven't
seen yet. The stadium is packed. Seventy-five
hundred people. Most wearing some form of electric
yellow. The team name is Thunder. Well, at least the
colour makes a little more sense.

Luckily for me, I manage to find my way to a familiar
face. Samantha flags me down. She is sitting with a
few of the other football team girlfriends. I assume
the rest of the team is probably dating cheerleaders. I
guess that is her friend group. They are just sharing

pictures over their phones the whole time. Samantha and I have barely talked the last month since I'm not working at the pizza shop anymore and she was on vacation. Dad is a big NFL fan, but I don't watch much. I would call my knowledge a general awareness of basic rules, and I know the superstars.

The crowd is loud before the game. Everyone chatting, but that dies down a few minutes before kickoff. The crescendo though as the opening kick takes place is impressive. The crowd is hanging on the ball in the air, and once the returner has it, the crowd explodes. You can't hear the person next to you. I want to talk to Samantha about her parents and the lipstick, but I can't find a quiet break.

We are on defence first, and the crowd never lets up. The Broncos are a good team, and they march down the field in short order to score an opening touchdown. The crowd has been hushed just as quickly as they had ramped up.

Now, we have the ball. These players look like men compared to my figure. We're not the same. Our ages may be similar, but there is some hardcore gorilla DNA out on that field. Trevor is lined up wide and on our side. I watch him closely. The ball is snapped. Trevor takes two quick steps and then lowers a shoulder, planting the guy in front of him into the ground. It's a running play. They sweep the ball to Trevor's side. After planting the first guy, he pushes another guy a few yards down the field. Overall, a modest gain. Next play.

The crowd is quiet. You can hear the Quarterback calling out signals from the line of scrimmage. Red. Red. Four. Forty-seven. Red. Hike! Trevor takes two steps and fakes dropping his shoulder to plant the guy again. With a quick ducking sidestep, he goes into high gear. There isn't a person near him. The ball is launched way up in the air. Trevor runs under it with ease. He barely moves his arms as the ball softly lands against his gloves fifty yards down the field. The crowd explodes again. He jogs the last twenty yards as if he has done it a thousand times already. He probably has. In the endzone, the big brute of a lineman named David comes up to him and lifts him four feet into the air, hugging him around the waist and playfully rag dolling him up seven feet into the air. People are jumping around in the stands.

Trevor makes two or three more plays like that. He is by far the best player on the field. The teams go back and forth for the next couple hours, trading multiple scores until our end comes out victorious.

Trevor is an athlete, Geoffrey is a singer. Erica and Caleb are just cool. What am I? A middle of the pack runner with a quarter-baked book idea. These people are so much further along than me. I want to catch up. After the game, Samantha and I track down Trevor. I commend him. It doesn't take long before I notice Samantha and him are gone. There are just too many people.

The Path of Business

ERICA has become the de facto project leader. She knows so much about the publishing process. Her uncle is obviously a smart guy, and she has taken an interest in his work. It shows. She is a natural leader too.

Business is also my favourite class by a long way. It is a combination of an awesome teacher, useful information, and getting to work with people I like. I wasn't expecting to like it as much as I do. Unlike my other classes, I feel like I am actually learning something almost every week in business.

The book isn't going to get written. We all know this. There is a concept, but we have no idea how to actually write a book. In that sense, the project is a little disappointing. That said, we still go ahead. Ms. Cooper says it takes years for most businesses to gain traction, so she isn't expecting to make a class of millionaires. Failure is part of the journey.

The group that's really taking this seriously is the "tomato" guys. They seem to be close to actually pulling something off. They might grow, process, and sell a "tomato" before the end of the year.

One of the reasons our group is struggling is some dead weight. I have no idea what these two people are doing. They come to class and just sit there looking at the wall. It is impressive how clueless they are. I guess not everyone can be a Geoffrey, but these two are a special breed of useless, needing constant spoon-feeding and incapable of independent thought. The only thing they seem good at is sharing memes. Every class they are showing me another one. Most recently it was the Forever Alone cartoons, which make light of the fact that most people who live their lives on the internet are destined to be lonely. Were they trying to show me a self-fulfilling prophecy? I have no idea what their motivation was.

We get to talking about the last party. Erica is so different at school. She almost has split personalities. There is this shy, nerdy bookworm who is a wealth of process knowledge and a budding master of business and English, then when you see her outside the electric yellow walls, this little devil comes out, tempting and mystifying.

The whole friend circle has taken to her. She eats lunch with us most days. With Ashley being such a flake, it is nice having Erica around. Ashley will be gone for days on end, and then, even when she is around, she doesn't say much. Erica is always around and easy to talk to. She said the last party took her like three days to recover from. We all agree that we went too deep. Although fun, next time we will go lighter. We can't be messed up for a half-week.

The other thing we talk about is Geoffrey. The talent show was just before the break, and it had us all looking at him differently. Geoffrey should have been in our business class. You could make a business around that skill. My novel idea is just that, an idea. His music is already a bankable skill. Not everyone knows about his mom though, so there is this complicated balance to asking Geoffrey for time. I know if he's playing for me, he isn't playing for his mom.

At the end of the day, I am really wondering if maybe business school might be a good choice. You can almost make anything into a business. I don't want to study books. In fact, I barely have any interest in reading books. What I want to do is create something and then get it out to the world. Business seems like it might be the proper vessel. If I can figure out the creation end on my own, the business side is the skill I need to learn. I don't tell anyone this, but I am really considering the change.

The Event

EARLY January. Cold. There isn't really a crowd. Don't sports have crowds? Football has a crowd. I guess running isn't really the main attraction of high school sports. In total, we have eight schools and forty runners. Maybe thirty fans. Probably all family.

Trevor hands me my team shirt. It matches my shoes and bands perfectly. We have the brightest school colours. There are some light blues. A black. Nothing too crazy, except ours. My warmup; twenty minutes of stretching and light sprints.

We all get ready. The starting gun. Everyone else sprints out of the gate. I never sprint early. There is a different energy to group running. You feed off it. It elevates you. Extra adrenaline. We are two minutes in, and I am bringing up the rear. The pack is starting to separate. People find their pace. The course is well marked. Officials stand at a few problem points here and there. They have bikes to shuttle ahead after clearing the back of the pack at each checkpoint.

Around the ten-minute mark is where I find my serenity. My thoughts disappear. The noise vanishes.

There is a runner ten metres in front of me. I close my eyes for a few seconds and focus on my feet. They start to feel lighter than air. I open my eyes. The gap is down to five metres. My eyelids crash down again. Dig deep. Turn up the tempo. I open my eyes. A few strides. The competitive drive in me takes over. The jets come on, and I blow past the other runner like he is standing still. I get there. The Zone. One foot over the next. Nothing else in the world matters right now. My skin catches fire. That tingle when you just break into a full-body sweat. It's euphoric and energizing. Now I am sprinting. Fueled by simplicity. Fueled by the THC that broke open some new pathways. Fueled by Geoffrey. Fueled by Erica, Samantha, and Ashley. Fueled by Dad.

That's when something completely unexpected happens. We come to a hill. It's a mammoth. Five blocks long. Twenty percent grade. I have been running hills for months. Apparently, that isn't normal. I didn't know. I just ran around my house, and there were hills. At this moment, I realize that hill times are different than street times. There is a bright yellow shirt just a little in front of me. On the street, I would have passed him within fifteen seconds, but on the hill, it is like he is in quicksand. One or two strides and he is behind me. I actually pass a runner from our team!

I finish fifteenth of the forty participants. Our team, first. I wasn't even the dropped score! Even though I had run the best time of my short career, Trevor had still beaten me by ten minutes, and it barely even looked like he tried.

Running Rock Star

SOMEHOW in my mind, I thought that doing well in the running event would make me a rock star. It did for one person, Dad. Another blind spot. Failure to really think things through. Why did I think the running team would change anything with Samantha or my social status? After lunch, I am at my locker.

Locker Girl: DO YOU LIKE HARRY POTTER I LOVE HARRY POTTER DEATHLY HALLOWS ONE WAS SO GOOD I READ THE BOOKS SO I KNOW HOW IT ENDS BUT I STILL CAN'T WAIT TO SEE THE MOVIE I WATCHED ALL THE HARRY POTTER MOVIES OVER CHRISTMAS BREAK TO CATCH UP THEY'RE SO GOOD THE FIRST TWO THEY ARE SO YOUNG IT'S LIKE OH MY GOSH I CAN'T BELIEVE WE WERE ALL LIKE THE SAME AGE WHEN THIS STARTED NOW THEY ARE OLD WHY DO WE HAVE TO WAIT A FEW MORE MONTHS I WANT IT NOW

My mind drifts away. I am just nodding, probably
throwing in the occasional "uh-huh" and "yes".

> **Locker Girl:** WHEN THE LAST HARRY
> POTTER COMES OUT WE SHOULD GO
> AS LIKE A GROUP ALL THE GRADE 12
> PEEPS IT COULD BE LIKE PART OF
> OUR GRAD PARTY THAT WOULD BE
> FUN HEY SPEAKING OF PARTIES DO
> YOU WANT TO GO TO BRAD'S PARTY
> WITH ME?

I don't fully catch that and just nod along.

> **Locker Girl:** OH MY GOSH THAT'S
> AMAZING I AM GOING TO POST
> RIGHT NOW.

I come back to Earth a bit.

> **Someone:** Post what?

> **Locker Girl:** SILLY YOU'RE GOING
> WITH ME TO BRAD'S PARTY!

I am? Who is Brad? What have I done now? I don't
even know her name and sometimes her talking
makes me want to throw up in disgust. It's pure fluff.

After class, I have my spare, so I make my way over
to the counsellor's office. It still looks the same as the
first day. One office is pristine and untouched. The
other is a mess of papers. Again, no one is there, so I
sit down and wait for a bit. Soon enough, Man Bun
eventually emerges from the corridor.

Kevin: I hear you did well on the running team.

Someone: Thanks. You're the first to bring it up.

Kevin: Running isn't the flashiest of sports. Keep it up. You're doing great for just a couple months.

Someone: I've got a question for you.

Kevin: That's usually why people come around here. What's on your mind?

Someone: Girls.

Kevin: Girls. Plural?

Someone: Yes. Plural.

Kevin: Okay. Elaborate.

Someone: So there is one girl. I worked with her over the summer and I felt like we had chemistry, but then when school started, she started ignoring me.

Kevin: The summer fling...

Someone: It was never even a fling. We just talked a lot. I thought she liked me. We seemed to be having fun.

Kevin: Some people are different people in different places. That girl might not be the girl you think she is, or maybe she is afraid to be that girl around her other friends.

Someone: Then there is this second girl. She is complicated. I don't know much about her, but she is amazing when we are one-on-one, and I like everything about her physically. She has the coolest hair ever. Her mystique is part of it.

Kevin: The enchantress.

Someone: There is another girl in one of my classes. She is smart, and she has become a close friend. I am starting to like her too. The fourth is why I am here though.

Kevin: Four! You are going to make me blush.

Someone: There is a girl at my locker. She talks my ear off, but I barely listen to her. There is just no connection. The other three, I can feel something. With her, nothing. The problem is somehow I have ended up going out with this locker girl.

Kevin: How does that happen?

Someone: I wasn't paying attention, the topic changed, and next thing I know, I had agreed to go to a party with her.

Kevin: First of all, you need to slow down. Ask yourself what you want then communicate that. It may be hard, but it's better to be honest and open. Speak your mind. Maybe go anyways just to be certain, but don't string her along. When you first meet, that is usually lust. It's quick and fleeting. Greedy. Self-centred. When you feel a strong bond quickly, be wary. It could be temporary. Try to take it slow. Love is methodical and giving. You have to work at it. It takes time. The first few months are often the hardest because love and lust are so similar. It takes a while to tell them apart. Pick the person you want to protect. Pick the person you can wear sweatpants with on the couch watching TV. Make sure you're not compromising your future and the feeling is mutual. Life speeds up as you get older. Years will snap by. You will wish time was slower like when you were younger. Enjoy young love.

Someone: Thanks.

My dad never gives me advice like this.

Someone: How do I know?

Kevin: You don't. You can't. You just have to use that brain of yours to guide you. It will tell you when it feels right. You can also trust your gut.

My eyes twinkle. Kevin is such a wealth of knowledge. Anything he wants to share is fine by me.

>**Kevin:** Can I change topics?

>**Someone:** Go on.

>**Kevin:** I was reading about trusting your gut.

>**Someone:** I have heard that before.

>**Kevin:** Everyone has...but what does it mean?

>**Someone:** It's just a feeling.

>**Kevin:** Is it though? Think about it.

My gears are turning.

>**Kevin:** So the theory is that the gut is alive with bacteria. These bacteria feed off what you give them.

I nod to show I am following.

>**Kevin:** Say you are eating bad. Your gut will be processing a bunch of sugars and fats. You will gain weight. Feel slow. If you trust your gut, you will listen as it sends signals to your brain. Hey dummy, get healthy.

Someone: Makes sense.

Kevin: So trust your gut means to make sure you are healthy. If your gut is unhealthy, change something. Your diet. Your schedule. Your behaviour. Trust your gut!

Someone: What does that have to do with the girls?

Kevin: Trust your gut. Which one makes you the most queasy? Which one makes you want to change your behaviour the most?

We just kind of get lost on that thought for a few moments, looking out the window. I feel older. Like what I have just been told is a secret that took years to develop and hasn't been shared with everyone.

Someone: How goes your running?

Kevin: I'm training for another race.

Someone: Really? Where is this one?

Kevin: Middle of nowhere. The Bigfoot Two Hundred.

Someone: The Bigfoot Two Hundred?

Kevin: You run around in the forest for two hundred miles in the dead of winter. It's savage.

Someone: How long does that take?

Kevin: Two days of solid running. You can take breaks and sleep, but if you do, someone else is running.

Someone: That sounds awful.

Kevin: The ones who make it are revered in the community as having an iron will. I want that.

Someone: When is it?

Kevin: Next winter.

Someone: A year?

Kevin: A year.

Someone: That is a commitment.

Kevin: That's why I love to run. It keeps your mind focused. My mind can get lost easily, so I like to focus.

Just a Regular Friday

I am looking for something to do. The day is dragging. My dad is out of town. He hadn't elaborated. Is it work? I just assume it is. He trusts me to be safe. Oops. Caleb is going to see his dad. So is Samantha. Ashley is basically missing, and I expect to see her on a milk carton soon. The slow methodical slippage of time. The anxiety of not having a plan. The hallway is its normal, ear-bleeding pre-lunch atmosphere. As I try to make my way through the hoard, a girl bumps into me.

>   **Someone:** Erica?

>   **Erica:** Indeed.

>   **Someone:** What are you doing tonight?

>   **Erica:** Nothing.

>   **Someone:** What if I said I was doing nothing?

>   **Erica:** I would say interesting.

Someone: Interesting.

We share a second of eye contact, both wondering the same thing.

> **Erica:** What about your dad?

> **Someone:** Nope.

> **Erica:** Nope?

> **Someone:** He is out of town.

> **Erica:** And you are alone?

> **Someone:** He does this sometimes.

She ponders something.

> **Erica:** Would you like to go see things?

> **Someone:** See things like what?

> **Erica:** Your past...

She says it with a wry smile. Her face changes. The nerd in her instantly falls away, and this confident creature comes out. Something primal and connected. Once you know Erica, you can feel the change in energy. It radiates. No one else in the hallway has any idea what we are talking about. They probably don't even know we are there. Yet in those few seconds, instant connection. Lifeforce aligned.

She reaches into her purse, a grin across her face, scribbling something across a piece of paper and then folding it up.

> **Erica:** Here.

> **Someone:** What's this?

> **Erica:** A clue.

> **Someone:** A clue to what?

> **Erica:** A clue you have to follow.

I start to unravel it.

> **Erica:** Stop!

She says it abruptly, as if I have broken a rule.

> **Erica:** Wait until dusk.

> **Someone:** What?

> **Erica:** You are not allowed to read that until the sun touches the horizon.

This girl...I am impatient. These games are hard.

> **Erica:** Trust me. You and I will have a night.

I fold the paper up and place it in my pocket. She smiles back at me. We are still getting to know each other. I have met Erica dozens of times. I have only met the Shaman twice. They are different people. The rest of the day drags even more slowly. I keep looking at the clock. I swear the hand are moving backwards. The urge to open the piece of paper and take a peek is intense. Every few minutes, the thought creeps back in. Impossible to focus on anything else.

Finally, the day is at an end. By the time I get myself home and have a snack, the sun is creeping down. It might be a little early, but the time feels right. My hand creeps into my pocket. My heart races. Slowly, I unfold the paper.

Meet me at the park where the old tree grows. Don't drive...run.

What does that even mean? I am clueless. My mind is racing with my heart. This is a riddle that must be solved now. How many parks could there be? I jump onto Google and put "old tree" in. It links me to some parks way outside of town. That doesn't seem right. I find three parks in the city close to our school. Nothing about an old tree. Time is ticking. The sun is crashing. What do I do? Then it hits me. I can run to them all. I put on my gear. Electric in the night.

The first park is a bust. The sweat dripping now. Two options left. Purple dusk as darkness creeps over the city and the moon begins to peek out. Heart racing, mind racing, time evaporating. I put the afterburners on. If Erica is waiting, I must get there. I can't leave her hanging. The second park is larger. The night brings an eerie vibe. I can't see more than a few feet. A combination of trees and darkness. I stop. Take a deep breath. Relax for a second. Let the park come to me. No sound though. Not a twig rustling. This can't be the place. Legs on fire, I take off in a dead sprint. This last park must be it. Watch for traffic. It's dark. They can't see me. My focus is gone. Careful sprinting isn't something I practice. The moon has come out. It's full and radiating light down on the path in front of me. I haven't checked my phone. No idea what time it is. I hope this is the right park. I hope she is here. I take my pace down a little as I approach, paying more attention to my surroundings. Connecting again. Let the world come to me. The running turns to jogging, then walking, then nothing. Me standing still. Time is ticking. Focus. Do I hear anything? Frogs and crickets. The hum of the city.

Listen harder. Harder. Then I hear it. A rattle. Just a half-second. The slightest shake. There are no rattlesnakes here. This is it. I start to creep towards where I think the sound came from, the moon providing enough light to make out shapes. Nothing is moving except me. Another rattle. Louder and closer. My eyes and ears both point directly to this old tree sitting in a clearing. It's not far. I stand, watching. Seconds go by. No movement. Slowly, creeping forward now, eyes laser-focused. Ears dialled in. Nothing. Mere feet from the tree, my walking pauses. This is the place. What am I supposed to do?

I stare at the tree. The little boy who stares at trees in the dark. From the sky, something falls. It's a piece of paper. I unravel it. I hear another rattle from above. I look up, but it's too dark.

Someone: Erica?

I say it so quietly, I barely hear myself. Nothing. After a few seconds, I make my way to the paper and unfold it. As I approach, the rattle picks back up. It's slow and methodical, but not stopping. I stop and look above me. The rattle stops. I glance around as the moonlight tries to pierce the branches, but I can't make out anything in the tree. As I turn, the rattle picks up again. I reach towards the paper, and the rattle gets more intense. As I unravel it, something falls into my hand. I know what to do. Without hesitation, I ingest. My heart racing, my mind racing, my eyes and ears focused. The rattle is exploding with noise. I just stand there, waiting, for minutes. The rattle starts to fade. I turn to look up, and it intensifies again. I stare through the branches. I can feel the source. Slowly, I make my way closer to the tree. Every step is accompanied by a little more intensity.

Someone: Erica?

Still, I whisper. Nothing. The noise stops.

Someone: Erica?

I silence everything. No more frogs, no more crickets, no more city. Pure focus. My eyes are closed. My ears guide me now. At least twenty seconds pass. I feel the wind. Then I hear it. Something climbs down the tree. I try and make my way around to see, but with every step the shadow creeps around the corner too. The moon's blistering glow reveals a silhouette.

Shaman: STOP!

I didn't know I was breaking a rule.

Someone: Erica?

I know it's her; I just want to be reassured. I can make out something that looks like the cloaked figure from our previous encounters. I can't make out a face in the night though.

>**Shaman:** This is not about Erica. This is about you.

My mind kicks up again.

>**Someone:** What do you want me to do?

>**Shaman:** I want nothing.

A slight shake to end the sentence. A brief pause from my end.

>**Someone:** I am confused.

>**Shaman:** I know.

Again, I pause.

>**Shaman:** Unclutter that mind.

Another shake.

>**Shaman:** Think deep inside.

Another louder shake.

Shaman: Focus.

Silence.

Shaman: Who are you?

The rattle is intense. It bounces around relentlessly for a few seconds. My mind is exploding. My head is spinning. My stomach starts to turn. Pain. The world is heavy and spinning. I can't hold it back. Something stirs inside. The rattle pulls it out. I feel the burn come up my throat at the speed of light. As I crouch down, I project pure bile onto the ground underneath me.

Shaman: Yes! Release.

Noise, relentless still.

Shaman: Keep going! Get it all out!

Time stops. It feels like an eternity. I don't just empty my stomach, I empty my soul. Once finished, I am exhausted, but I also feel light. Free. Something has been released.

Someone: I think I need to lie down.

Shaman: Not here.

She whisks me away. I stumble around with her guiding me. Her arms on my shoulders. Her stomach pressed up against my back. Steering me as if I were a vehicle.

>**Someone:** Am I okay?

>**Shaman:** Only you know that.

>**Someone:** I don't understand.

The words are getting harder to get out. They burn with bile and slur with time. Proper sentences have become a struggle.

>**Shaman:** Of course you don't. Just keep walking. I will guide you.

Under the pale moonlight, she keeps me going. One foot at a time.

>**Shaman:** What are you thinking about?

>**Someone:** Getting home.

>**Shaman:** Don't worry about that. I have that.

I stop thinking for a bit. Then I start thinking of who I used to be. Alone. Afraid. Lost. Scared. Anxious. I start to feel a blackout coming on. I get lightheaded. The Shaman props me up.

>**Shaman:** What happened?

>**Someone:** I thought about my past.

Shaman: Good.

She pauses. Holds me tighter with one arm and grabs something with her free hand. Then lightly the beads begin to knock against the wood once again.

Shaman: Keep thinking.

I oblige. Deeper I go.

****

I am at my old school, in my old town. I am in a room. It's a cooking class, I think. The teacher is counting us off into groups. I am terrified. Cooking with new people isn't what I look forward to. She lands on me and directs me to three of the popular girls. Great. I have even less to talk about now because I can't tell you a thing about trendy teenage girls and fashion. Oh my. What do I do now? The teacher is blabbing about the cooking lab, but I can't focus. All I can think about is what do I say once we start cooking. Five minutes go by. Everyone starts to get up and go to the stations. I make my way over. The teacher is still barking orders. I recognize one of the girls in my group. It's the scissor girl from elementary school. We don't talk much though. I never did trust her after that incident.

Out of nowhere, scissor girl runs out of the room, tears running down her cheeks. Twenty-five eyes on me in an instant. I didn't say anything. They don't know or care. I am guilty without even doing anything. The room begins to swirl. I fade away. I wake up in the nurse's office. She has her back to me.

It doesn't take me long to find myself. Within an instant, I am gone. Straight for the door and back home.

On my way out, I run into one of the jocks, and he shoulder checks me to the ground. He is going to kick me, but I think he sees how weak and broken I am, so he leaves me. Eventually, I pick myself up. What am I going to tell Dad? What a mess. I don't even say anything. I think. For twenty minutes, thoughts bounce around my mind, trying to remember exactly what had gone down. Finally, the front door is upon me. Dad is home. I knew he would get a call, but I thought I would have an hour to sort it out. I knock. I don't know why. Courtesy and respect for Dad? Nothing. I creep in, and I hear him coughing in the bathroom. I didn't know he was sick. It sounds horrible. Deep chest coughs. I just go and sit at the table. He comes out of the bathroom and looks startled.

> **Someone:** Are you okay, Dad?

> **Dad:** Don't worry about me. What happened?

> **Someone:** I don't know.

> **Dad:** The principal said you touched one of the girls, then blacked out and ran away after. I came right home.

Did I touch a girl? I don't remember that. No.

> **Someone:** No. Absolutely not!

Dad: Well, why did you come home? You can't do that. You scared everyone.

Someone: I wasn't thinking.

He scowls at me.

Dad: Clearly.

Someone: Sorry.

Dad: This one needs more than an apology.

He is thinking. Hard. Deep.

Dad: You are staying home for the rest of the week. I need to think this one out. Just...just...I don't know.

****

All of a sudden, I fade back. A hand is rummaging in my pocket.

Someone: Wwwwhhhhaaaattt'sss goooooooiiiinnnngggg ooooonnnnn?

Oh my. I am having trouble.

Shaman: Relax. I have this.

She gets my keys out and guides me to my bed. She doesn't know which one, so we open all the doors. She wraps me in a blanket.

Shaman: You were gone. I saw you leave
Earth. I don't know where you went, but
don't be afraid to go there again. Follow it.
Embrace it.

She makes sure I am extra tightly wrapped. It feels
really good. Warmth. Comfort. She sits in the corner.
No lights on. Slowly tapping her beads against the
wood.

Shaman: Sleep. Think. Relax. Who are
you?

I fade away again with the soothing rattle.

****

I am in a room. It's an office. I am in a pretty average
chair. The building is pretty old. The office is well
kept, but boring. Really small and tight. The smallest
office I have ever seen. Claustrophobic. It doesn't
look like it is supposed to be an office. Beige walls.
There is a nameplate on the desk. Dr. Drum: Child
Psychologist. It's just me. Waiting. Nervous. Afraid.
Unsure. It feels like forever. Waiting for this stranger
to try to "fix" me. She looks like a librarian. It is the
glasses and greying hair. Too much makeup. Red
lipstick. Almost like a clown mask for the world. She
smells of smoke and bad perfume. In this small
office, it is inescapable and putrid. She looks me up
and down. Examining me.

Dr. Drum: Look. You think you are special.
You think your problems matter. I've got
news for you. We all have problems. You

don't even know what a real problem looks like. You are young, entitled, and spoiled.

Wow. That was direct. I don't even agree. I don't think my problems matter. I want to just disappear, and other people keep pushing me into the light. Plus, she doesn't even know anything about me. My mom. My blackouts. Maybe I do know what a real problem is. Maybe she is the one who is spoiled and entitled. I sit in silence.

> **Dr. Drum:** Nothing. Figures. You can't handle that you are not the centre of the universe. Well, tell me about the recent incident.

I ponder. Is this even worth my time? I am here for Dad though.

> **Someone:** I really don't remember it well. I was nervous because I didn't know my group. Next thing I know, one of the girls is crying and I wake up in a different room.

> **Dr. Drum:** Is that all?

> **Someone:** That's all I got.

> **Dr. Drum:** That's not the story I heard.

> **Someone:** Enlighten me.

> **Dr. Drum:** Don't give me lip.

I scowl at her, and she scowls back. It's a scowl standoff.

> **Dr. Drum:** The story I heard was you touched the girls behind. That is so inappropriate. Then you don't even apologize. The poor girl was devastated.

I don't remember that. If I did, it was an accident.

> **Someone:** I know her. She lies.

> **Dr. Drum:** Prove it.

> **Someone:** I can't. I just know.

> **Dr. Drum:** She was absolutely violated.

> **Someone:** Look. That isn't what I did. It's ridiculous to accuse me of being some pervert. Come on.

> **Dr. Drum:** I don't know. You don't come across as respectful.

> **Someone:** It's mutual.

The scowl-off again.

> **Someone:** You believe her!

> **Dr. Drum:** You are already on shaky ground. Who is everyone going to believe?

So professional...she isn't even listening.

> **Someone:** Are you actually going to help me?

> **Dr. Drum:** There is no helping you. Grow up. The world doesn't owe you anything.

I sit there, angry. Stewing. Brooding.

****

It's warm in my blanket. The noise is gone. The Shaman is gone. It's just me and my thoughts. Hours have gone by. Who am I? Why didn't I remember this? How many times did I see Dr. Drum? What did the Shaman want me to get out of this?

Across the room sits my moon lamp. Softly glowing. Warm. Inviting. A soothing beacon to the new home we have. The little dimples and imperfections are beautiful. I study it to the point of a mesmerizing trance.

I pass out again. This one resembles a hibernation though. No flashback. Twelve hours of sleep. When I wake up, it is like I haven't slept a minute. It is a strange feeling, all the forgotten memories crashing back in. Later that day, Dad comes back. I have to ask him.

> **Someone:** Dad, who was Dr. Drum?

He raises an eyebrow.

Someone: What?

Dad: You hated her. I believe you said, "I think she goes home at night and sits in the corner facing the wall."

Someone: What do you know?

Dad: You went four times. You complained she was useless every time. When I told you we were moving, I think you were happy to get rid of her. You are doing so much better anyways.

Why can't I remember her? This is so weird.

Someone: What did she tell you?

Dad: She said you were struggling to admit you had made a mistake and open up. It was a weird situation. I don't know what the truth is. There are so many layers.

He looks at me, puzzled. I am still missing a piece, but I leave it at that because I think I am worrying him with how little I remember.

Someone: Thanks, Dad. Where were you?

Dad: Nowhere special. Did you have a good weekend?

Someone: Indeed.

Erica the Shaman

ON Monday I have business class at the end of the day. It also means I will see Erica. I need to talk to her. What was that? Who was she? Another slow day. A reoccurring problem. My focus is on the social side of school. I have been basically ignoring assignments and then cobbling them together at the last minute because my time is being pulled in so many directions. It is a new problem, having too many friends. Having to manage all the relationships. Choosing which ones I could spend time with and when. Right now, Erica is the friend I need, but she is also elusive. I don't know much about her. She seems to have real wisdom. Rare wisdom. I like that. During class, I keep looking over. She doesn't look back for quite some time as if she knew I wanted to talk, but was going to make me wait. Really think about what I say next.

The topic is interesting. Online Marketing. I wish I could be more focused because I am sure there is a ton of useful information. Finally, almost near the end, she looks back.

Erica: Can you walk me home?

Someone's Story

I know what that means. It is code for let's talk.

> **Someone:** Sure!

Class ends. We quietly gather our stuff and go to each other's lockers.

> **Someone:** Erica, we are friends, right?

> **Erica:** Of course. I like you.

> **Someone:** How much?

> **Erica:** No. Not like that. Do you?

> **Someone:** Not really. You fascinate me. Confuse me. I just wanted to be sure it was mutual.

> **Erica:** It's mutual.

> **Someone:** You are so quiet and "normal" around school.

I give air quotes to normal.

> **Erica:** I was taught to compartmentalize early. It's a skill.

> **Someone:** Why are you helping me?

> **Erica:** I think you have potential. There is something inside you. Deep. You don't even know it yet. I see it.

Someone: What do you mean?

Erica: Don't take this the wrong way, you are a little simple, but once you figure out how to get past whatever is holding you back. That thing in you, it will explode into something. I feel it. I see it.

I ponder. No one has ever said anything like that about me. Maybe Kevin.

Someone: What did you give me?

Erica: My tool.

Someone: This was different.

Erica: Shaman's secret.

Someone: Where did you get it?

Erica: My family is very progressive. We use tools the general public is afraid of. I was taught how to use those tools the right way. My family was adamant they teach me rather than some crude, horny teenage boy. I am so glad they did.

Someone: Your parents give you this?

Erica: Not exactly. They trust my judgement. They want me to share. Spread the skill. Plant the seed. They didn't expressly give me this, but they gave me the path. I choose how and when to use it. It was

my older brother who really showed this to
me.

Someone: Wow. My dad would never let
this fly.

Erica: It's not something you talk about with
everyone. Be careful. Again,
compartmentalize.

Someone: How do you compartmentalize?

Erica: You've already started. Managing
relationships without telling everyone
everything and then keeping track of that so
you don't make a mistake.

Someone: That sounds hard.

Erica: You have to practice. It's actually
easy for me, but everyone is different.

Someone: Why play the game?

Erica: That's not how the journey works.
You have to earn it and learn it. That was
probably a weird night, wasn't it?

Someone: Absolutely.

Erica: What did you think about?

I am not sure if she is ready. Does she know the
extent of my counselling? What if I tell her about the
"touch"? I get kind of quiet.

Erica: It's okay. That wasn't for me. That was for you. I hope you got what you needed. I hope you are finding yourself.

She has no idea.

Someone: Thanks so much. They don't make them like you.

Erica: They don't make them like you either.

We smile. I reach in for a hug, but she steps back.

Erica: Our friendship is business.

Someone: Here is a question: What do you do if you are dating a person you don't like?

Erica: I have no idea, but I just wouldn't...that is a waste of time.

Everyone I ask has basically told me the same thing. Time to face the music.

Not My Party

AN Erica-style party is more my thing. Small social gathering, doing fun things with friends. Cool. I'm in. When you start to get to fifty people, I get quieter. There is no intimacy. Too many airheads. I am dreading this, so I show up thirty minutes late. When I get there, it's pretty typical. Like what you might see in a movie. Red plastic cups full of various types of booze. People doing stupid things in the back yard. Way too many people in the house. The occasional couple that sneaks off to a quiet room. Most of the guys are in jeans and polos, trying to impress the girls by leaving the hoodies at home. It's just noise and annoying frat boy laughs all over the place. Why do I not like hearing people laugh? This place just makes me spin. I don't like the busyness. It reminds me of the first day of school. Not my idea of fun. I try to just catch my breath. Once Locker Girl finds me, I will probably have a headache within minutes, so I better enjoy this brief period now.

Surprisingly, I know most of the people. Not well, but I get around at school. I can talk for two minutes with just about any of them, but I don't want to, so instead I just park in a corner and observe. I hear the words "winning" and "tiger blood" at least a dozen times. No idea why.

Samantha is deep in conversation with Trevor. She is her flirty self. Watching it from afar makes me sick. It's the same girl I have spent hours talking with at Bambino's, but I am not on the other end. I just keep watching. Eventually, Samantha starts laughing hysterically at something said then kind of playfully slaps Trevor.

Locker Girl finds me. I kind of want to ask her name, but at the same time, I think she has told me already a dozen times so I am afraid to bring it up. She talks my ear off, as expected. My head is spinning. Then the strangest thing happens. Five or six people burst out into song. They are all chanting "Friday".

Then, even stranger, almost the entire room joins in. Locker girl is amongst them. I don't know what is happening. One of the kids pulls out a phone and cranks a YouTube video. Rebecca Black takes the lead and sort of raps.

The video almost feels like a parody. I can't tell if it is serious or a joke.

Then the entire room, everyone but me, joins in at the top of their lungs for the chorus. That was the first ever time I had heard *Friday* by Rebecca Black. It became a staple years later.

I think I have lost a few brain cells. I can't take it. It is similar to some of my previous incidents. The room is getting small. The people sound hollow, and their voices are echoing. It is almost like falling. The laughter is louder. Spinning from Locker Girl talking my ear off and spiralling from the insanity I have just been a part of, I tell her this is a mistake. It goes awfully. She cries. Around this time, I also notice Trevor leaving for a room, followed by Samantha. Quickly, I make my way for the backyard. Need some air. Need to get away from the eyes.

A pleasant surprise, Ashley is there, sitting on the edge of the garden wall. She is smoking a joint, and when she notices it is me, she quickly offers it up. I declined because I am driving later and the Shaman taught me better. Ashley always seems to show up when I need her. It is strange but welcome. She is glowing right now. I don't say anything, but her outsider, loner energy is really hitting home. I want what she has. The freedom. After a bit of talking, she reassures me life will move on, and that most people probably will forget about this night in a few weeks. I love the way she doesn't care about Rebecca Black. She doesn't care about who likes who. She is so different than the normal people at this party.

Fight

I am rummaging for a textbook. Locker Girl comes up. She puts in her combo. Takes a book. Then leaves. Not a word. I feel awful. Even though I hated it when she spouted off, that was her. To see this dejected, quiet girl makes me sad. In English, she sits as far away as she can.

In addition to being ignored by Locker Girl, I am also the target of a meme. The eyes are piercing. Two people would look at me. They would talk softly to each other. One would pull out their phone. They would look at it for just a second or two. Then they would look back at me with giant smiles. As if I didn't feel bad enough. The meme is Scumbag Steve and the caption says "First date with girl at party", then at the bottom it says "Dump said girl at same party".

The lunch bell rings and I am on my way to find a seat when some guy comes and grabs me. It is Caleb. He is panicked and without food, which is very uncharacteristic of him. He shouts to follow him. I chase him out to the field behind the school where a large group has gathered into a circle. The sky is grey and ominous. The group is yelling. There is no one else in the fields because everyone has gathered here. A light rain begins to fall.

It is already underway. Geoffrey is a small guy, and this animal is rag-dolling him around the circle. Caleb is fighting through the crowd, me close behind him. It is all happening so fast. I know the brute. It is David from the football team.

Geoffrey is trying to fight back, but there is a massive size difference, so at best he can dodge and run. It isn't long before he is face down on the ground. The rain is now coming down hard. Mud covers the ground, and Geoffrey is basically wearing a layer of brown.

Caleb is right in the middle of it all now. He calls out to me for help. I am frozen. David punches Caleb right in the face. It drops him instantly.

The savage raises his giant leg and crashes it down onto Geoffrey's hand. You can hear the bones shatter as the size fourteen boot mashes them into the mud. He finishes the stomp by shouting, "Play your guitar now!"

Caleb jumps back to his feet and pushes David away in order to try and give Geoffrey some shelter. Blood is pouring from Caleb's nose. He calls out to me again for help. Everything is spinning. I am still standing at the edge of the circle, frozen with anxiety.

Caleb's leverage is only good if they aren't moving. David charges forward like he is on the football field and shoulders Caleb to the ground like a runaway freight train. The force sends Caleb flying, and he lands in the mud, looking up at me. I can see the question in his eyes: Why don't you help? It's Geoffrey. You know the story.

Geoffrey is still writhing in pain, grasping at his wrist to try and take weight away from his mangled hand. About this time, a few teachers show up. The crowd, wet with rain, disperses fast, and I stand frozen for an extra few seconds, trying to get my head and feet to communicate. My stupid, frustrating brain just won't do what I want. I think about Geoffrey. His mom. It hurts that he might lose that playing time. I think about Caleb. I let him down. I could have stopped them maybe. I could have thrown myself in the middle. Trevor might have listened to me and jumped in. David might have listened to Trevor. I did nothing. Then the thought that really gets to me. I remember all that bullying from my old school. I had forgotten most of it. It hurt. All the popular, athletic kids who picked on me. I spent most of my early days in high school trying to hide from people. I hated that person, and I thought I had put him behind me. Having him come back is frustrating and terrifying.

The rest of the day is spent piecing together a secondhand version of what had happened. The "girlfriend" of the monster had been talking to Geoffrey. Just a few weeks ago, she would have been out of his league, but coming off his chilling performance, he had instantly elevated his social status. From what I gathered from her friends, they were just talking about what else he could play. Nothing more. Something was completely misinterpreted and within minutes, Geoffrey found himself being pushed outside by three or four of the players from the football team.

I am so sad I failed Caleb and Geoffrey. I hate my anxiety. It freezes me when I am needed most. I am so mad at David. What a terrible thing to do. So braindead and shortsighted. How could Trevor like that guy? Shortly after the fight, one of the younger students comes up to me. He is in grade eight but could pass as ten years old.

> **Kid:** Hey.

> **Someone:** What? I am busy.

I am fumbling around, still scatterbrained and spinning.

> **Kid:** You know Mr. Geoffrey, right?

Now he has my full attention.

> **Someone:** Yeah.

> **Kid:** What they did was so mean. I like Mr. Geoffrey. He is in my drama class, and he helps everyone.

> **Someone:** I know. Pretty awesome dude.

> **Kid:** I know something.

I am puzzled.

Someone: What are you talking about?

Kid: About Trevor and the big guy.

Someone: You mean David?

Kid: The guy who stepped on Geoffrey.

Someone: David.

Kid: I was taking a number two a few weeks ago.

Someone: T.M.I.

Kid: They came into the bathroom together.

He pauses, gathering himself. I look at him like I might know where this is going.

Kid: I picked up my feet because I didn't want them to know I was there. They talked about girls. Trevor said something about just meeting a new one. He said she was like a dead fish.

Someone: What did he say about Samantha?

Kid: Who is Samantha? I don't really know what it means, dead fish.

I am furious, and I am not telling this kid what it means.

215

Kid: That's not all.

Again, he pauses.

Kid: They finished up, went to wash their hands and that's when I heard something.

Someone: What?

Kid: They touched.

Someone: Did you see it?

Kid: No. But I heard it.

Someone: What did you hear?

Kid: I don't know, but it was something.

I think back. The butt slap at the game. The way Trevor treats girls. The messaging in the library. The way he just talked down on Samantha. It doesn't seem farfetched.

Someone: Are you sure?

Kid: Positive.

Someone: Stay safe, and tell no one else what you just told me.

Shortly after that, I run into Samantha and she asks me to meet her after school. Too much happening at once. Ahhhhh!!!!!!!

216

The Roof

AN hour after class, me and Samantha meet. She is wearing school-branded sweatpants, grey with Mountain Dew school lettering, and the Studio Ghibli shirt I bought her. She usually dresses lighter. She just feels and looks heavy.

> **Someone:** What's up?

> **Samantha:** Have you ever been on the roof?

> **Someone:** No.

> **Samantha:** Come on.

We head down the hallway.

> **Someone:** You must have heard about the fight?

> **Samantha:** Everyone did.

> **Someone:** Is Caleb alright?

Samantha: His face is busted up pretty bad, but his friend...

Someone: Geoffrey. I know him too.

Samantha: That sucks. Caleb is not happy with you.

Someone: I know. I am not happy with me.

Samantha: He said he called out for you twice, and you stood there confused. Like you were in a trance.

Someone: It happens. I wish it didn't...

Samantha: Did you feel like you weren't in control?

Someone: Yes!

Samantha: I know that feeling...

She leads me to a corner I have never been to, looks both ways and behind us, then opens a door that leads to stairs. There is a lock, but she has the key. I am not going to ask how she got it.

Someone: Did you hear about the party?

Samantha: Yup.

Someone: So you know what happened to me there?

B.A. Bellec

Samantha: Yup.

Someone: Where were you?

Samantha: I don't want to talk about it.

I know anyways. We go up a few flights of stairs and emerge on the roof. She makes her way to the edge and looks down.

Someone: Careful.

Samantha: Don't worry. I have toed this line before.

Interesting. Why would she have been on the ledge, three stories up at the school? As she stands at the ledge looking down, she just looks beautiful. There is a light breeze pushing her away from the ledge. Her hair and clothes wave ever so slightly in the wind. It's as if the breeze were the only thing holding her back right now. I slowly make my way over. Heights aren't my thing.

Someone: It's pretty high.

Samantha: I have stood on higher.

Another interesting comment.

Someone: Caleb told me about your dad a bit.

Samantha: Did he?

219

Someone's Story

Someone: He mentioned the lipstick.

Her expression goes from sad to sadder.

Samantha: I remember that.

Someone: Why didn't you bring it up at work? It's good to talk about things like that.

Samantha: Is it?

Someone: I think so.

Samantha: I just bury it.

She looks off the ledge again.

Someone: Can you get down? You are getting me worried.

She turns and steps off.

Someone: What's up? You seem off.

Samantha: Do I?

Someone: You do.

Samantha: It's that obvious...

She pauses and contemplates her next words.

Samantha: I need something from you.

Someone: Sure, I guess.

Samantha: You do one for me, and I will do one for you.

Someone: I am listening.

Samantha: I know you are in the social graveyard right now because of the party. I have had a recent change in status again myself. I will take you to the dance. You have to do something for me after.

I stop. This is exactly what I wanted. I just didn't know how to ask. Lucky me?

Someone: Really?

Samantha: Yup.

Someone: Yes.

Samantha takes a step towards the ledge and looks down again, then comes back to me and gives me a hug. She is so warm. What a strange couple of days. I broke a girl's heart, betrayed two of my best friends, then won the dream girl? I want to talk more about Trevor, but not yet.

Grad Dance

ONE of the last events of the year for grad is our dance. This is a prepaid event so the food and drinks are free. I don't need to run the door or anything special. I have never been to a dance, too many people, and I was awkward so it was hard to find the courage to approach anyone.

My social life is complex. Caleb, Geoffrey and Erica have all given me the cold shoulder because of my stupid brain. Ashley is in ghost mode. Kevin is off doing a run. I have been relegated to eating lunch alone most days. Our business class is super awkward. Locker Girl hasn't spoken to me since the party. The only thing really going my way is that Samantha has finally started talking to me again. I don't know why, but she has.

Samantha is stunning when I pick her up from home. She is wearing a tight black dress that covers most of her arms and legs to hide her tattoos. Her hair is freshly dyed. Black with vibrant red streaks. She told me she was wearing black and wanted me to do the same. I don't really have lots of clothes, so I picked up some cheap black clothes from a thrift store.

When we show up, the event is already well underway. We spend a few minutes walking around, gathering our footing in this new setting. A slow song comes on, and she drags me out to the dance floor. I awkwardly stumble around on her. When the song ends, we briefly part ways. I run into Locker Girl while getting a drink. She doesn't say anything. I do learn her name though, Amanda. Another person was talking to her, and I might have been listening more than I was leading on. Caleb is around the snack table munching on anything he can get his hands on, but he quickly moves somewhere else when he sees me coming.

The highlight might be Geoffrey. He generates a buzz when he shows up. It might be a sympathy date, but he formalizes the fears of the big brute, David, by stealing away his girl. Cast and all, he has everyone astonished by the absolute ten hanging off his arm. I wonder how many other people know about his home life though? Unknown to me, he has gone viral. A student had recorded his performance from the talent show and uploaded it, where it has apparently generated thousands of views.

I notice Samantha talking to Trevor. They get kind of heated. She doesn't yell, but there is a bit of anger. Then she comes over to me. We make our way back to the dance floor. She grabs my hips and pulls me in close, then rests her head on my shoulder. She seems exhausted by something. She whispers in my ear.

> **Samantha:** Remember when I said I needed your help?

Someone: Of course.

Samantha: Trevor and I have been off and on for a while.

Someone: I kind of knew that.

She is almost ready to buckle and fall to the floor. I can feel her head resting on my shoulder with the weight of an entire universe behind it.

Someone: What is it?

I see a tear roll down her cheek.

Someone: Just get it out. Come on.

Samantha: I am pregnant. I don't know how it happened.

Someone: I know.

Samantha: No. I mean I am on the pill, so I don't know how it happened. I must have missed one. Trevor isn't...he isn't that kind of guy to me. He is fun for a few minutes, but I don't see him as part of my long-term plan.

Someone: You want me to kill Trevor?

Samantha: No.

She snickers. The weight is lifted a bit.

Samantha: You're the only person I have told. I want you to help me with the, you know, clinic visit.

Someone: Oh. Are you sure?

She looks over at Trevor.

Samantha: Positive. Don't tell Caleb. If my mom finds out, I'm dead.

Someone: Don't worry. He and I are not talking anyway.

Samantha: That's right.

Someone: So you and Trevor are done?

Samantha: Done.

Strange times. It's like the world has been turned upside down from a few weeks ago.

The Clinic

I don't tell anyone what I am up to. I meet up with Samantha right after school the next day in the parking lot.

Someone: You still sure?

Samantha: I am.

Someone: Okay.

I get the sense she doesn't want to talk about it. I think she wants comfortable, but not too familiar, in order to distract her from the traumatic event she is about to go through. I don't disagree with her decision. Trevor is not the kind of guy to stick around.

Poor Samantha. She is about to change her life either way. Life or death. The decision belongs to her. She keeps the child, and her entire life is on a new path. She does what she is about to do, and her entire life is on a new path. There is no right decision. She can't see the future. This is heavy.

I try to make the wait fun. It's the best I can do. We discuss anime. I have watched all of her recommendations. *Akira* is a classic. *Ghost in the Shell* has strong *The Matrix* vibes. She knows her anime. She is currently rewatching *Naruto*. My *Naruto* exposure has been from the two doofuses in business who keep showing me running *Naruto* memes. I know nothing else. She gives me a quick overview.

The clinic is small. They eye me like I am the reason. They know nothing. I help her through the paperwork. Before long, she is gone. I am left alone to ponder why she picked me. She has girlfriends. Trevor did the deed. Caleb is like a rock. Yet she went with me.

It takes a little longer than I thought. Her mood is down, but that is to be expected. I have had a thing for Samantha since the day I saw her. Watching her make this tough decision only further cements my respect for her.

My life is a ball of stress. After I drop Samantha off at home, I ponder the last few days. I come back to one emotion, anger. I am so mad at David and Trevor. I couldn't bring myself to tell Samantha what they said about her, and I am still mad about Geoffrey. Instead, I create an anonymous social media account, and I make a "David + Trevor ?" post. There is more on my mind still that I can't say, so I write it out into a letter for Samantha. It talks about our first encounter and how I have always hoped she liked me. Then I start to get into how lately she has been giving me signs back. How I feel compelled to finally confess.

I put the letter into her locker the next morning. Waiting is the hardest part. I know she will probably text as soon as she has read it. The first few hours go by. Nothing. It is the second period. I try to catch her in the hall but don't. Finally, I get a text: *Can we talk?* I leave class right away. We meet outside.

    Samantha: The letter was beautiful…

She pauses. I know I am not going to like the next words.

    Samantha: I don't like you like that.

What does that mean? She likes me? But not like that? Friendzone. Ouch. I just went with her…

    Samantha: I have been going through a lot the last few months. I am just not ready for anything serious. I want to be friends.

How can we be friends now? I don't say anything. I just put my head down in embarrassed shame.

    Samantha: Look. I am sorry. The dance and all the talking. I get it. It's just…

I don't want to hear it.

    Samantha: Wait.

Too late. I am already gone. I feel like a complete idiot. I thought the signs were real. I thought what I felt was real. How could I be so wrong?

Ashley

S HORTLY after my Samantha incident, Trevor pulls me aside.

Trevor: Dude, you have been flakey lately.

Someone: What do you mean?

Trevor: Haven't seen you in class. Didn't come to our last team meeting. You going to finish the English assignment? You know we run again this weekend?

It feels like an attack. What he doesn't know is I already did finish the work. Now I am wondering if I should give it to him. I like to watch him squirm.

Someone: Don't worry about me. You know what you did, right?

Trevor: Oh. You're mad about your little buddy...are you the one...did you...?

He stops and thinks for a minute. I think I know what he is thinking. It has to do with the anonymous post. There is no way they could trace it to me though. Prove it. I give him my poker face. My mind goes to his other question. I love to run. At least I used to. Come to think of it, I haven't even thought about running the last month. Does running matter? I'm not going to go to the Olympics. At most, I would be lucky to get onto a college running team. The "therapy" I get from running is fading.

Someone: Hey Trevor, one more thing.

My heart is pounding. Fear and anger. Before fear would win. I am usually too afraid to act. Not this time. Now my anger wins. I hate this guy that much.

Trevor: What?

Someone: I quit. Write your own assignments.

He says something under his breath as he walks away. If feels good to be free of Trevor, but this only lasts for a few moments. Problem is, now I have almost nothing. I try to track down Kevin. He is busy. I think about talking to my dad, but he hasn't been home lately.

There is one more person. She has been a ghost herself. She might not even be going to school anymore. It feels like months have passed without seeing her. I find Ashley.

Ashley: Sup.

Someone: I'm going for coffee.

Ashley: Sure.

She takes an earbud out. So Ashley. When the choice is class or anything else, she goes with anything else.

On the way to coffee, I start to tell her everything from the last few months. I don't know if she cares, but she listens, which is better than I am getting anywhere else. We go and order our blonde roasts. I have one question on my mind from a long time ago. The present. I have seen so little of Ashley, I never got to actually ask her about it.

> **Someone:** Do you remember Erica's last party?
>
> **Ashley:** Of course.
>
> **Someone:** When I left, someone had put something in my shoe. Was it you?
>
> **Ashley:** Yes.

I knew it...that was a really good experience.

> **Someone:** Thanks.
>
> **Ashley:** Happy to help.
>
> **Someone:** Where have you been?

Ashley: I am done with school. There is nothing more for me there.

Someone: Are you dropping out?

Ashley: I don't know. I can probably still pass the finals.

Someone: You should.

Ashley: I know. The place just bores me to death.

Someone: Me too. I have messed everything up. I just want to get out of that place. These last couple of months can't go fast enough. You know what's been happening.

Ashley: Not really.

I keep filling her in on Geoffrey, Caleb, the Trevor incident, and the mistake I made with Samantha. It is actually lots now that I have it all in front of me.

Ashley: Is your place empty?

Someone: My dad's at work all day.

Ashley: Let's get out of here. We got to stop somewhere first.

Interesting. Ashley is so impulsive, who knows what is on her mind this time. We have barely been at the coffee shop five minutes. I have never seen her place though, so I am curious to see where she takes me.

We drive across town. We arrive at the posh neighbourhood. Seven bedrooms, four baths, three car garage kind of homes. I had no idea she was this rich. She finally tells me to stop. It's a bloody mansion.

Someone: What does your mom do?

Ashley: This isn't my mom's place.

Someone: Where are we?

Ashley: It's a secret.

I don't know what that means. Anyways. I pull up and park on the road. We can't get through the gate. She runs in and is barely gone three minutes. She gets in the car, all smiles. When we get back to my place, she pulls out a couple of little smiley face treats. She puts one on my tongue. I swallow. She quickly consumes one herself. I don't think it was her first. I think she already took one back at that place. She leaves me the bottle. It has a bunch more smiley faces inside. I hide it away so my dad won't find it. We talk until whatever it is kicks in.

I am having trouble standing. My legs are like jello. Ashley pushes me onto the bed and says relax. She leaves the room for a few minutes. When she comes back, she kind of stumbles around herself. What did she give me? I am pretty out of it. All I remember is fading in and out. Everything is spinning. I keep grabbing my head and holding it for minutes at a time. I feel like I am going to vomit again. It is awful.

234

Not the joyful experience the last few times were. This time...it is...painful.

****

The little tight room. Silence for minutes. The smell of cigarette smoke and putrid perfume. She is fumbling around with her files on her desk.

> **Dr. Drum:** Talk to me about religion.

> **Someone:** I don't have an opinion. Not a factor in my life.

She doesn't like that answer.

> **Dr. Drum:** I think religion is rules, structure, and community.

She looks at me smugly.

> **Dr. Drum:** You need some order. Structure. Something your mom didn't provide. You are lacking some critical skills.

> **Someone:** Look, I follow the rules society lays out. Isn't that enough?

I can see her eyes roll slightly. Another answer from me that she disagrees with.

> **Dr. Drum:** If you don't think you need religion, talk about your mother.

Someone: What does my mother have to do with religion?

Dr. Drum: Structure. Order.

Someone: Didn't Dad tell you?

Dr. Drum: I want to hear it from you.

Someone: I don't know my mom. She left when I was young. No clue where she is or what she does. You are not going to find any structure or order there.

Dr. Drum: I think you need some influencers in your life. Something to replace your mom. That's it about your mom? A couple sentences? Seems kind of strange, doesn't it? You barely have an opinion on religion and on your own mother. Maybe religion would give you the structure your mother didn't. What about your grandparents?

Someone: I can't make her come back. My grandparents…

I pause and stare right into her eyes.

Someone: Grandpa died a few years ago. Grandma doesn't speak English. I have never met anyone from my mom's side of the family. What else do you want to know?

Dr. Drum: You are talking about your dad's side of the family?

Someone: Yes.

Dr. Drum: How often do you see Grandma?

Someone: Never.

Dr. Drum: Why?

Someone: I just don't. I tried. She doesn't seem interested in learning English.

Dr. Drum: Why can't you learn to communicate with her? This is just like your view on religion. It's so selfish. You are missing my point. How do you feel about your mom leaving? About not being able to talk to Grandma?

Someone: I don't know.

Dr. Drum: You should feel something.

Someone: I don't really feel much. My mom is gone. I don't mind the life I have. Grandma is in her care home and a person more capable then me looks after her. I am nothing special. There is nothing I can do to help either of them.

Dr. Drum sears a glare at me. She is frustrated by my answers. I am frustrated by her questions.

Dr. Drum: Do you feel responsible for your mom?

Someone: Me? For what?

Dr. Drum: Her leaving.

Someone: Absolutely not. Her choice.

Dr. Drum: I think you should take some of the blame. People don't just up and leave. There are factors in play. To think you are innocent is ridiculous.

Tension fills the room. I can feel my blood start to boil.

Someone: To think you know what another person is thinking is ridiculous.

We stare at each other. This is war. Who blinks first? Maybe no one blinks ever again.

Someone: If she cared, she would have said something. She would have tried to reach out again. How dare you blame me!

Dr. Drum: So you don't feel responsible for your actions?

Someone: It depends.

Dr. Drum: I am just saying I see a pattern.

B.A. Bellec

Eyes lock again. No blinking allowed.

> **Dr. Drum:** You had the incident at school. You know what happened?

Now I am at a roaring boil.

> **Someone:** I do.

> **Dr. Drum:** Let me enlighten you anyways.

I clench my fist.

> **Dr. Drum:** You assaulted a poor girl in class.

She can see the fire in my eyes.

> **Someone:** She lied.

> **Dr. Drum:** No, she didn't!

Dr. Drum returns fire like a pirate ship shooting a cannonball from a few feet away.

> **Someone:** You are not thinking about what happened to me. All the bullying. The trauma I have to go through. For the rest of high school, I am the kid who touches butts.

I exhale my breath like a dragon breathing fire. Deep. Far-reaching. No words though. Just fire breath. Eyes locked.

239

Someone: It's not true!

Dr. Drum: I had to treat that girl. She was devastated.

Someone: She is a liar. She tricked you.

Now I shut my eyes. The room is molasses thick with tension. By shutting my eyes, I feel it even more.

Dr. Drum: There is no helping you.

Someone: ENOUGH! HOW DARE YOU BLAME ME!

Like an explosion. All the rage. All the fire.

Someone: YOU ARE BLAMING ME FOR MY MOM LEAVING AND FOR THAT GIRL'S LIES!

Dr. Drum: Calm down.

I almost hiss her quiet like a snake about to spit venom.

Someone: YOU ARE SO BAD AT YOUR JOB!

Dr. Drum: What do you know about my job?

Someone: I know you keep blaming me as if I am the problem.

We get quiet again.

> **Dr. Drum:** She has a name.

> **Someone:** Why does that matter?

> **Dr. Drum:** The girl has a name! Where is your empathy?

Now Dr. Drum is starting to show cracks.

> **Someone:** I don't know it and don't care. I can't believe what is going on. Honestly!

Laser-focused eyes again.

> **Someone:** If I liked her, I would know her name. If anything did happen, it was an accident.

> **Dr. Drum:** Then why didn't you apologize?

> **Someone:** I didn't do anything wrong. Why didn't she apologize?

> **Dr. Drum:** Really?

> **Someone:** Really...

> **Dr. Drum:** You are hopeless. You will never be anything more than a parasite if you don't learn to hear feedback.

The venomous exchange ends.

Someone's Story

****

I spring to my feet. Cold sweat drips from my head, soaking my clothes and bed. Was that a dream or a memory? Ashley is gone. People keep disappearing. It is a brutal night, fading in and out of these horrible flashbacks to my old life which is becoming my new life again. I feel so alone.

Stress Exorcism

TRUTH is harsh. In the morning, I pull out my phone. I do something I have never done. My life unravelling, I go back to my source of wisdom. I call Kevin. I ask for help. I do what Dr. Drum wanted me to do. I admit I might be the problem.

> **Someone:** Kevin?
>
> **Kevin:** Hey, man!
>
> **Someone:** You free?
>
> **Kevin:** Of course! You have never called.
>
> **Someone:** So I have been having these...

I don't know the word.

> **Kevin:** Memories?
>
> **Someone:** But they are like dreams.

Kevin: Go on.

Someone: I remembered my first counsellor again. An incident at my old school.

I pause because remembered isn't right.

Someone: I didn't remember. That's not the right word. It was like I cleared the memory from my mind. You remember the Neuralyzer from Men in Black? Somehow, that happened to me. Then it came back.

Kevin: How did it come back?

I don't want to tell him about my experiments.

Someone: They just did. Like dreams. And I feel like my life is turning into that mess again.

Kevin: Are you sure they are real?

Someone: I talked with Dad a bit. He seemed to know what I was talking about, so I think they are real.

Kevin: Why are you telling me?

Someone: I want to talk about Dr. Drum and the incident.

Kevin: Was that her name? Okay. Describe her a bit.

Someone: Old. Stubborn. Insensitive. Cheap perfume and cigarettes.

Kevin: It's not good to hate. Release her. Don't give her power over you. What did she say?

Someone: She kind of blamed me for my mom leaving and she sided with this girl who was a pathological liar. It cost me years of bullying. I had no friends.

Kevin: That's serious.

Someone: Right.

Kevin: I need more.

Someone: I just had a couple of flashbacks. I remember hating her. I remember wishing I had never agreed to go. I remember learning almost nothing. I remember pain. Fear. Depression. Anger. It just baffles me that the truth was lost. That no one believed me.

Kevin: Truth doesn't always win. Life is hard like that sometimes. You have to find a way to navigate those cloudy patches.

Someone: If it wasn't for you, I would be falling apart on the ground right now. Spinning in circles.

Kevin: Well, different people, different strokes. Some people look at symptoms. I am more holistic. What makes the machine tick? Start there and work back. If you just sniff around the edges fixing minor problems, you are basically applying band-aids over and over again. Not my style.

Someone: Right. That is kind of what I felt. She blamed me before I could even tell my side. She was just trying to get me out the door. You always want to give me a bigger solution to a small problem.

Kevin: It happens. Lots of people bounce around for a while before they find a therapist they like. If you clash, the visits can be as poisonous as the reason you went.

Dr. Drum's visits felt like poison.

Kevin: Tell me about the girl.

Someone: That's hard.

Kevin: Why?

Someone: I don't know what really happened.

Kevin: What do you remember?

Someone: I remember being anxious about being in her group and then kind of blacking out. I guess it's possible I touched her while I was blacking out, but it was an accident if

246

it did happen. It's not the malicious assault
she described it as.

Kevin: Let's focus on growing. The future is
bright. You are still here because you are a
fighter. You are strong. You have more tools
now. The past happened. Use it as a tool, but
move on from it.

Someone: I guess.

Kevin: I want to give you one more tool.
Something I call a "stress exorcism". I want
you to write down everything you screwed
up. Everything that is causing you stress.
Then once you have that list, see if you can
find something that was causing each item
on the list. How many are connected? How
many are coming from the same stressor?
Can it be eliminated? Or, at least, can you
change your behaviour to diminish the
effects?

Someone: Then what?

Kevin: It's up to you. Once you have the
answers you want, light the page on fire and
go for a run. Save it in a shoebox. Do
whatever makes you happy with it.

Someone: Hmmm….

Kevin: Meditation.

Someone: Meditation?

247

Kevin: Yes. Mediation. There are many forms. In fact, anything you are passionate about can be a form of mediation. When you lose yourself in a task, the rest of the world falls away. That is meditating. I would say that jogging is my usual form. Use it to clear your mind. Refocus. Writing is another. A nice long bath. Yoga is really popular.

Someone: What do you focus on?

Kevin: Nothing at first. Clear the mind. Then choices. Life is a series of choices. All my paths and choices led to a scenario where I have a beautiful wife and daughter. In order to provide for my wife and daughter, I need a house. To have a house, I need a mortgage. To have a mortgage, I need a job. The job itself is a means of keeping my wife and child happy, so then it becomes about finding something I can enjoy. I thoroughly enjoy coaching developing minds through hard scenarios. This is deeply satisfying. I am getting an intrinsic value from the job beyond the pay. The pay satisfies the needs of my family, and the job satisfies the needs of my mind. I balance them out with some jogging as meditation. That's my life equation, if you will.

I like this. The life equation.

Kevin: To balance the equation of life is an impossible task though. There is no right answer. You make the answer. My life equation is unique to me specifically. At best, I can recommend you to be mindful. To be mindful, you should meditate. See life from other perspectives. Once you achieve mindfulness, then your decisions are rational and balanced. At times, there are many paths in front of us. There is always an answer, but there aren't always right answers. Sometimes the paths are too many to evaluate. Sometimes the outcomes are cloudy. Sometimes there is not enough time. Then your task becomes to mitigate the risk. To try to take the path with the least resistance and then find a way to reconcile the decision. Use the stress exorcism to see the bigger picture, then use meditation to answer the questions.

Someone: Sorry.

Kevin: Why are you sorry?

Someone: I feel like I let you down almost? Like I got weak and forgot what you taught me.

Kevin: Don't be sorry. The fact you called shows you are getting closer. Keep doing what you are doing. You are on the right path.

Instead of paying attention in class, I work on my stress exorcism. I keep writing about the mistakes I have made. Every few minutes, I would write another. The list gets pretty long. The flashbacks. The last few months. Once I start to look at them all together, I notice a trend. Most of my stress is because I am trying to please others instead of doing what I need. I keep sacrificing myself. I am giving pieces of myself to everyone else and my past. In the end, most of this is wasted. I am not getting what I need back to move forward. I am pleasing the wrong people. I am standing in my own way. I need to get right with Caleb, Geoffrey, and Erica. After school. I think about burning the page, but don't. It feels special. Like I have finally put together a few pieces to my puzzle.

I put on my electric yellows. I run for me. It is the first time I have run for me in months. Meditation. Deep in thought. Lost in my own mind.

Amends

GEOFFREY is at his house. His cast is off. He is in his basement, working on some music.

Geoffrey: Long time no talk!

Someone: No cast.

Geoffrey: No cast. Just a few days ago.

Someone: Man, I am so sorry.

Geoffrey: It's fine, man. You didn't even do anything. Caleb was mad at what you didn't do. That's a bit harsh. I hate that place anyways. You hear what they did to David?

Someone: Nope.

Geoffrey: Nothing.

Someone: Not surprised. No bad blood?

251

Geoffrey: No bad blood. You and me are fine.

Someone: The girl from the dance?

Geoffrey: She didn't know me. That was just a social thing.

Someone: So it was just the dance.

Geoffrey: She felt responsible. I felt obligated to make her feel better. Honestly, total airhead.

Oh, Geoffrey...

Someone: How is everything at home?

His smile recedes.

Geoffrey: Man...it's not good. My dad is getting worse. He is never home. Mom is not getting better either, so the clock is ticking. I just started playing for her again a couple nights ago. Got some cool new song ideas.

Someone: I wish I had tried to stop the fight.

Geoffrey: You probably would have been crushed.

Someone: I absolutely would have...but I don't have a person back home waiting for me to play guitar.

Geoffrey: That's sweet, man, but it's some nice creative fuel. If nothing happens to you, what do you sing about?

He shakes my hand with his previously broken hand. It's stronger now. Perhaps this was a blessing? Caleb and Erica are in my business class, so at least I don't have to go looking for them. On the way, I see Trevor walking in the hall. All these eyes are glancing over. I bet he wishes he is invisible. I know the feeling. The topic today is Toyota. Ms. Cooper is giving a presentation on their efficiency.

Ms. Cooper: Who here knows Toyota?

She looks around the room. We all are giving this puzzled look because of course, we all know Toyota.

Ms. Cooper: Toyota is a fantastic business study. They developed a system called TPS, Toyota Production System. It's fascinating and a gold standard to benchmark manufacturing against.

She puts up a slide.

Ms. Cooper: Muri is overburden; Mura is inconsistencies; Muda is waste. The goal is to remove Mura, but to ensure it is done in a way that doesn't cause Muri, because Muri generates Muda.

The students all have puzzled looks on their faces.

Ms. Cooper: It may seem a little confusing, but think about it. What if you were working twenty hours a day on a school project. That is overburden. You will start to develop inconsistencies and waste. You may have to work a few long days, but the more you overburden, the more you see the bad results creep in. In your groups, I want you to talk about your three M's.

Caleb and Erica are sitting a few rows over now, doing everything to distance themselves more from me still. This is going to suck, but I need to address this and move on. I haven't even been coming to class, so I think they are a little surprised to see me. I hate the feeling. I have two people I like that had been nothing but friends. I had abandoned them. It had left me broken. We couldn't talk. I just want to apologize, but finding the words and strength has been hard.

Someone: Caleb. Erica. Come here.

They both look at me.

Someone: Look. I know I made a mistake. I was out of balance. I made some horrible decisions. I just want to say I am sorry. My anxiety is a problem. I am working on it. It's a me thing.

They are still both just looking at me.

Someone: I talked to Geoffrey. He got his cast off. He is cool. We are good.

They are still both just looking at me.

> **Someone:** Come on, guys, give me something. I miss you.

Caleb leans over to Erica and whispers something. She nods. He hands her a Starburst, and they both unravel one. They are just looking at me. It's getting kind of awkward now as they chew on their Starbursts.

> **Caleb:** We accept your apology.

I almost cry. I wanted them back so badly. To hear them say yes is such a weight off my shoulders.

> **Caleb:** Remember who your real friends are.

> **Someone:** I do. It just took me a while to realize what was gone.

He flips me a Starburst. These people are awesome. That's why they are my friends. Even when you make a horrible decision, they are there, waiting to give you a second chance. The kind of people we wish we all knew.

> **Someone:** So like…are we partying?

> **Erica:** Oh, we are definitely partying.

> **Caleb:** What do you think about this Toyota stuff?

> **Someone:** Dude, I like it.

Caleb: Right. Doesn't it make sense?

Erica: Like way too much sense.

Someone: Why don't other classes teach us cool stuff like this?

Caleb: Totally. I love this class.

Ms. Cooper: Okay. Does anyone want to share?

I raise my hand.

Ms. Cooper: What do you have for us?

Someone: I hate waste. It's just something I see fast. Waste bothers me. I am clean and organized. I eliminate the distractions from around me. I have a pretty small wardrobe. I have a few hobbies that I am passionate about and that add tremendous value to my life. I don't let papers accumulate. I don't let important tasks go unaddressed. I hate anything that is a time-suck. If you're thinking about something a lot, but not acting. You are potentially wasting that time. If you are waiting on someone else, you are potentially wasting that time. Once you are aware of the waste, then you can reassess. Reprioritize. Own your own path instead of being a prisoner to the process. Say you have an English assignment. It's really bothering you, but you are getting nowhere with it. You don't have the time to pick it

apart and proceed. What are you doing that
is causing your time to not be available?
What are your goals? Which thing supports
your goals, the paper? Or the other thing?
The answer may be to let the paper go.
Sometimes, failure isn't avoidable. It must
be managed. A small defeat on one
assignment does not define you. There is
always risk involved. Having a clear mind
will help you see the risks. Maybe your dad
will take your car. Maybe you will lose a
friend. Maybe you lose your spot on the
team. Why? What did you gain from the
loss? If you have two tasks fighting with
each, the ability to achieve a greater goal
through the management of these little risks
is what will define you. Muda.

Whoops. I went too deep. I think there are some jaws
on the floor. I usually only hear things like that from
Kevin. He is spilling over into my day-to-day
conversations.

> **Ms. Cooper:** Fantastic personal assessment.
> The 3M process doesn't just apply to
> making cars. You can use it for just about
> anything. I almost don't even think I need to
> show the next slide. You explained that so
> well.

She goes to the next slide anyways.

> **Ms. Cooper:** Kaizen. That is the word for
> continuous improvement. The ability to self-
> assess and ensure the goals and processes

are optimized. The English assignment was a fantastic example, where making a small sacrifice could result in a large long-term gain. Manage day-to-day processes with a specific set of long-term goals in mind.

My life is starting to feel balanced again. I have the right people in the right places. There is one other person I need to talk with. Ashley is last. The drugs had to slow down. She needs help too. She is disappearing for weeks on end and starting to suck me into her rabbit hole. She isn't answering, but now I have a place where I think she might be.

When I get there, I just walk in. Rich people. They don't even lock their doors. It must be nice living in a place where all your neighbours are millionaires. I yell and hear nothing. The house is huge, but one person has to be here. They wouldn't leave everything unlocked and go out. I start checking the rooms. I find a guest room and the master bedroom. There is a sign that says "Go Away" on a door. I figure that sounds like Ashley. She says this isn't her house, but maybe it is. Maybe this is her room.

I creak the door open. Ashley is lying on the bed. It looks like there has been another person here too. If there had been, they were gone now. I poke her. Nothing at first, then her arm slumps down limp. I softly say her name. Nothing. This time, a little louder. Still nothing. Then I notice the needle on the bed-stand. Panic sets in. I shake her. She is gone. I go find a house phone and dial 9-1-1. I don't want to use my cell.

Operator: 9-1-1, what is your emergency?

I can't speak. I just hold the phone.

Operator: Hello, is anyone there?

Still nothing.

Operator: If you can't speak, press any number, one time for police, two times for medical.

I press twice.

Operator: Okay. We are tracing the number. Stay on the line and we'll be there shortly.

I put the phone down and run.

Determination: Daylight

DAYLIGHT just begins to emerge over the horizon. It's a long night when you run in the dark. The eighty-eight on his chest reflects the sun as he strides away. Homestretch now.

A beacon flashes. It's another runner. They have put up the flag. Not everyone has an iron will. The runner with the eighty-eight takes a second to give this fallen comrade his water and emergency foil blanket. Onward our eighty-eight goes. Once he starts running again, it isn't long before he clears the forest. He takes a few steps and then lets out a primal scream. It echoes through the mountain.

With each step, the sun rises a little farther. Sore, bleeding, broken, yet energized. Battle-tested. It doesn't show on the outside. It's inside. Scars from past lives hidden away from the world under his armour of skin all project onto the sky. The giant kanban board that is his mind, sorting out the things that really matter.

The snow is dissipating. The ground becomes flat. The hard part is behind him. He could coast to the finish line and call it a good day, but that isn't the man he is. Instead, even after days of running, he slams his foot into the ground with even more enthusiasm than the first step he took when this race began. This battle is over. He won. He knows it. Now he obliterates expectations. His eyes are closed. They have been for minutes. It doesn't change a thing about his pace. He could run blind. His feet have become one with the surroundings. He has removed all other obstacles from the equation.

Left foot.

Right foot.

Left foot.

Right foot.

Left foot

Right foot.

Repeat times a million. No worries. No problems. No anxiety. No pain. Just feet doing their thing. His mind is recounting his entire life. He is living untethered. Limitless. Deeply meditative. A rare smile can be observed if you inspect his face close enough. He is proud of himself. Something he struggles with.

Reality

NOT knowing what to do and in a panic, I call an emergency meeting at Brown Bean. It has been a long time. Of course, they are all going to show. This is why I had to win them back. Once there, I pick up five blonde roasts and head for my spot. It doesn't take long.

> **Erica:** Hey. Oh, you got drinks. What is it?

Does she not know? Come to think of it, I don't think I have brought her into my blonde roast army.

> **Someone:** It's blonde roast. The best coffee on earth.

> **Erica:** The best coffee on earth?

She takes a little taste. She doesn't need direction. She knows how to taste something. She is refined. I watch her let the coffee roll around on her tongue. She has her eyes shut, really trying to be one with the flavours.

When she opens them, she makes eye contact with me and gives me a small nod. This is when Caleb and Geoffrey show up.

> **Caleb:** Been awhile since we had coffee.

> **Someone:** My bad.

> **Geoffrey:** It's all good. We're here now.

> **Caleb:** I see Erica started without us.

> **Someone:** She's never had blonde.

> **Caleb:** Oh my.

> **Geoffrey:** How? How could she go this long knowing you, without having blonde roast? It was pretty quick for me.

> **Someone:** I was lost. It made me a shitty person at times. I wish I could have been more aware.

They all kind of look down. There is a raw truth in that statement that hurts.

> **Someone:** That's behind us now. I needed to talk to you guys. Aren't you wondering why there isn't one more?

> **Caleb:** What do you mean?

Someone: Shouldn't there be one more person?

Caleb: Do you have a new girlfriend? I thought you just always wanted two cups of coffee. You are acting weird, man? What's the emergency?

Geoffrey: Ya. What's up?

Someone: Come on. Erica isn't the only girl we hang out with.

Caleb: Ya, she is. And she is awesome.

I guess I haven't been paying attention, but I think Caleb and Erica have something going. The way they just made eye contact. How they have been spending class time together.

Someone: Ashley?

Caleb: Who?

Someone: You're screwing around.

Caleb: I am not.

Someone: Geoffrey? Erica?

They are all looking at me like I am crazy.

Geoffrey: Are you okay?

Someone: You're telling me you don't remember the girl with white hair? Who came for coffee with us? Who sat with us at lunch? Who saw Harry Potter with us? Who goes to our school?

Caleb: You are scaring us.

Erica: What's wrong?

My mind is racing. I am trying to process. How could they not know Ashley? This is impossible. She might be dead for all I know. It's like I am living in a parallel universe where she never existed. The room is spinning. I feel it closing in on me. I panic again, and I run for my car. I probably shouldn't be driving, but I have to get home. I need my bed. I need to process.

Caleb: Wait!

Erica: You can't go. We need to talk.

They try to follow me, but I am too fast. All that running has paid off. I can escape almost anyone. Somehow, I am able to drive my car home. When I get home, I look for proof. She has to be real. Do I have anything? The present. It had notes. I kept it too.

Relentlessly, I rummage around in my dresser until I find it. I look meticulously, and then something hits me once I examine the notes really hard. The writing. Now that I know Erica, it is definitely her writing. How? What? There must be something else. She left me drugs. A big bottle of something. I find it. There is no sign of her though. Anything else? I can't. Who else saw her? Just my friends? Maybe homeroom? I can't breathe. It's bad. It's getting really tight. The room closes in. It spins. I crawl into bed.

My failures. Running. Samantha. Ashley isn't real, and I am a joke who can't keep it together. I remember Drum and my mother. What I did to Trevor. My haunted past is crashing in, and it hurts. Real pain. Not breaking a bone. No. Pain of the mind. Pain you can't escape.

The bed is too soft. I fall out of bed and lie on the floor. The floor is hard. It feels safe. I just want to get as low as I can. Give me a hard surface that I can let go on. Give in. Release it all. I am shaking as I reach down and grab something from my pocket. Everything fades away. I hear banging. I am in and out. Calling for me. I think it's Caleb, but I am not all here. There is a buzzing in my ear, and when I fade out, the buzzing gets really loud and I get a white flash. I am moving. Heavy and weightless at the same time. I can't hear anything except ringing. Another white flash. Intense buzzing. This time, everything stays black.

Clearing the Fog

BEEP.

Beep.

Beep.

Why am I hearing beeping?

Beep.

Beep.

Beep.

The blackness starts to give way. I open my eyes. It burns. It's so bright. Everything is hazy. My thoughts are still a fog. I moan, and Dad gets up quickly to my bedside.

> **Dad:** Oh, thank god. You had me scared to death.

I don't answer, but I move to acknowledge I hear him. Tubes and drips all over the place. I just give him a look that shows I acknowledge the words.

Dad: What were you thinking?

The buzzing comes back. A bright white flash. I pass back out. This time, I wake up and my head is absolutely pounding. There is a doctor standing over me.

> **Doctor:** Hey fella, you gave us quite a scare. Do you have any idea what happened?

I shake my head side to side very subtly.

> **Doctor:** Your friends saved you.

Tears form in my eyes slowly and then roll down my cheeks. I thought I had heard Caleb.

> **Doctor:** You took a lethal dose of MDMA laced with Fentanyl. You only had a thirty-minute window to flush your system. Your friend broke down the door to get you out. They called the ambulance. You're going to be okay. Rest.

It's all such a blur. I haven't even gotten to Ashley yet. Lifting off years of fog isn't for the faint of heart. It hurts. It hurts so much I almost lost it all, but for the first time in a long time, I am starting to think clearly. Feel and hear better. Retain. To anyone living life in a fog, work to clear the fog. The clarity is worth it. Seeing for miles beats seeing right in front of you.

The Padded Room

I am deemed high risk. The last few days are really hard to process. I tell them all about Ashley. It is brutal. I have to accept she isn't real. What does this mean? I can barely decipher truth from reality. My mind is a twisted mess. I don't know how to deal with stress. I thought I did, but only now am I was realizing just how blind I have been.

Ashley is starting to make a little sense. My previous experience with bullying and lack of friends, combined with my anxiety and introversion caused me to invent a friend to fill in the gaps in my life. She usually only had shown up when I needed her. She was a reflection of the worst parts of me. I wonder what Kevin would say. I hope he comes soon.

I don't get much freedom. They are watching me almost twenty-four hours a day. After a few days, they let visitors come. Caleb comes first.

Caleb: Wow.

Someone: I know.

Caleb: Wow.

Someone: You saved me, right?

Caleb: I guess so.

Someone: Come here.

I give him the biggest hug I have ever given anyone besides Dad.

    Caleb: You going to eat that?

My lunch is still on the tray. Some sad vegetables and a meat product.

    Someone: All yours.

Caleb grabs the fork and digs in.

    Caleb: We should have talked more. I shouldn't have held a grudge. We shouldn't have given you the drugs. Erica feels awful.

    Someone: It's not her fault. It's my own fault. My problems. She has to come.

    Caleb: She will.

    Someone: What are they saying at school?

    Caleb: Not much. We aren't talking. They just said you are sick and left it vague. I did tell Samantha. She will come soon. You had her pretty devastated.

Someone: Thanks.

Caleb: Ashley?

Someone: Apparently, I got some real problems.

Caleb: No one's perfect. Tell me the story.

I proceed to tell him everything I remember about Ashley. He fills me in, showing that most of the Ashley behaviour had been just me. I had twisted everything. Ashley is really me acting out. It is hard to stomach. I am hoping for Kevin, but Erica comes by the next day.

Erica: I just want to apologize. I had no idea.

Someone: I had no idea.

Erica: I should have been more careful.

Someone: You couldn't have known.

Erica: Honestly, it sounds like an amazing story.

Someone: I guess it is.

Erica: Like maybe a story you should write about.

My mind fires again like Kevin just told me something useful. I love that feeling, and it has been too long.

Someone: Can you get me something to write with?

Erica: Of course. Anything.

She leaves and comes back with an iPad pretty quickly. Less than thirty minutes.

Erica: Get better.

Someone: Thanks. So you and Caleb?

Erica: He is great, isn't he? So happy we all found each other. I brought something else.

Someone: Oh, really?

She reaches into her purse and pulls out one of those camping-sized mini boxes of Cinnamon Toast Crunch, a plastic spoon, and a small milk. That takes me way back. I eat it, and I tell her my Ashley story just like I did for Caleb. This time I take notes though. She stays for a few hours.

I am alone again. Reconciling. Then I hear the doctor talking to Dad. I don't think they know I can hear them.

273

Doctor: Your child has some fairly advanced mental health problems. Is there a history in the family?

Dad: Actually, yes. His mother.

Doctor: Elaborate.

Dad: His mother was in a really bad car accident. She was six months pregnant at the time with our second child. The child didn't make it. She spent months in the hospital. She was never the same after that. She turned to a life of pain medication, and then other things, and I left her. It was so long ago.

Doctor: Do you know where she is now?

Dad: No, I moved on.

Doctor: There is another thing.

Dad: What?

Doctor: The girl, Ashley, she isn't the only one.

Dad: What?

Doctor: There is another.

Dad: What are you saying?

Doctor: He had a fictitious relationship with a school counsellor named Kevin.

Dad: What?

Doctor: We checked the records. There is no Kevin working at Riverside High. Your child claims Kevin had been mentoring him since the move.

Dad: Hold on.

Doctor: I know. It's a lot to take in. I would call this one of the most developed cases of schizophrenia I have ever seen at this age. This usually doesn't start until early adulthood. This may have been the first time. We can't know for sure right now. We have as many questions as you do. Cases like this are rare.

Dad: How did they miss this? He was in counselling already once?

Doctor: It's hard to diagnose. It usually takes a big incident like this for the truth to come out.

Dad: Where do we go from here?

Doctor: I think you also need to tell him your secret. This is not the time to hold that back. He is safe now. We can help him.

Dad: Are you sure?

Doctor: Go on.

Dad comes into the room. I'm probably ghost white. How could Kevin not be real? He taught me everything. They're lying. I know Kevin is real. He has to be. His advice was real. It helped me. Didn't it? How could this be? Ashley was just starting to make sense. I just want to feel fine, but my mind keeps on telling me lies. I am as lost as ever. The room is spinning, but I keep it together. What is this secret?

Dad: I think you heard that?

Someone: I did.

He has a weight on his shoulders. Something heavy. Just like Samantha.

Someone: Am I going to be okay?

Dad: Yes. These are great doctors. They will figure this out. That's why I moved here. The best doctors in the world.

Someone: I thought you moved for work.

Dad: Not exactly.

Whatever is on his shoulders is pressing down even harder, and just like that, another epiphany crashes into me. All that coughing...

Dad: Kiddo...

The air in the room is getting heavy.

> **Dad:** I moved here, to help fight…

His eyes are getting watery.

> **Dad:** Cancer.

What? No. How? When? Why? No. No. I feel so blind. Why hadn't I been paying more attention?

> **Dad:** I should have told you, but you already were having the blackout problem. I didn't think you were ready. I thought I would beat it.

> **Someone:** You thought you would beat it?

> **Dad:** I thought I would…but the doctors are not giving me good news. It's not regressing.

> **Someone:** What are you saying?

> **Dad:** I am saying that I might not be around too much longer. You might have to go live with your uncle.

My world is falling apart. I reach out. We hug for minutes, both crying. Once he leaves, I start to write. I write everything about Kevin and Dad I can think of. This story just got bigger. They just became huge pieces. Everything they did with me the last year now has a hidden meaning, but it is locked away inside me. I already had Ashley, but this new story…it is surreal. I feel like an alien that doesn't belong on this planet. How can this much be broken? What can I do? How do I make this all make sense? How do I use this? Life is crumbling in front of me.

Healing

SOMEONE that used to mean the world to me is in front of me when I wake up. There they are. The red streaks. The dragon tattoo. She is sitting in the chair looking at something on her phone. She hasn't noticed I am awake. I just look at her. Not too different than the first day I saw her when she was standing outside the shop. She just has that girl-next-door vibe that, even after everything, I still just want to get to know her better no matter what happened between us. Instant, unexplainable connection. She looks up and sees me.

Samantha: Dude.

Someone: I know.

Samantha: You could have talked to me.

Someone: I didn't know.

She processes that statement.

Someone: What do you know?

Samantha: Caleb told me little bits and pieces.

Someone: Do you have any questions?

Samantha: No. I came here because I wanted to tell you something.

Someone: Go on.

Samantha: One of the reasons I couldn't keep what we had going was it felt too real.

This was great news. It validated what I thought at the time. What she had been hiding from me.

Samantha: I am going to tell you something that no one knows, and I mean no one. When I was in grade eight, I cut myself a lot. I had been seeing the counsellor because my mom was worried. Cutting was the only time I felt alive.

She is opening up to me, finally. After an entire year trying to get to this place, I have finally gotten there. I just had to throw myself through the washing machine of life.

Samantha: It started as just one, then I would do more. Go deeper. I was so embarrassed I was cutting myself, I wanted to cut myself more. I felt numb when I didn't cut myself.

She then looks up, deep into my eyes. The look she gives me, nobody is who they seem to be…

> **Samantha:** The last few times, when I looked into your eyes, I saw too much of me and I started to feel it again. I have emotional spikes. They come out when people try to get close. I have to keep everyone just on the other side of the fence. Whenever they try to climb that fence, I put the spikes out, then I run. Always. Every time.

Her head is down. She is telling me things only a few people on the planet know.

> **Samantha:** My spikes came out. I had to let you go because I was scared…for both of us.

I think I get it. I feel it too. Maybe that's the thing I felt all along. Maybe it isn't love. Maybe our connection is that we are on the same broken plain of existence together. Maybe that is love?

> **Samantha:** Even today. With the spikes gone, the feeling is still there. We can't though. I can't. I still have my demons. Look, I will always like you, but I have to let go of the things I like for their own protection. I am a monster. I am not ready.

We have a toxic mix. We need to keep growing, and we can only do that apart. The timing just isn't right.

> **Someone:** Can I see?

281

Samantha: They're hidden.

Someone: Where?

Samantha: Under my tattoos.

It all makes sense. The long sleeves, the wrist tattoos. The relationships with Trevor and Josh. They weren't asking her deep questions about life. She is covering up a haunted past too. She can't be alone with her thoughts because the voices in her head are so dark. I think about Samantha and Geoffrey. Two people who got dealt bad hands. One of them sits and just stews on all the negatives, afraid to really dig in. The other takes the negatives and tries to turn them into art. Uses them for inspiration. Be better.

I can't bring myself to talk about Dad yet. There is just so much happening. It is too fresh. I need to deal with my own wounds before I can start to unwind the rest.

After Samantha, there is one more person I want to reconcile with. I need to talk to Kevin. I close my eyes and I imagine his office. The clean desk. He is sitting in his chair. Trendy blazer, not buttoned up. Bun in full display. Sides freshly shaved down. Well-kept beard. Perfect teeth. This time, it is different though. There is a bit of a fog. Him and his desk are clear, but the rest is blurry and fading. This is imaginary and I know it.

Someone: You're not real.

Kevin: What is real?

We pause and ponder for a few seconds.

> **Kevin:** I am as real as you let me be. Anything and everything is real. Any work of fiction starts in someone's imagination. When do you call it real? When they make the movie? When they write the first word? Or is the moment something becomes real actually the second it creeps into your mind? Does having the thought make it real? Did it feel real to you?

> **Someone:** What am I supposed to do with this?

> **Kevin:** Use it. You can let it be your crutch...or you can let it fuel the fire. You can take this and turn it into something special.

> **Someone:** How?

> **Kevin:** That's up to you. You define you. You have to figure that out. Manage your time on this planet better.

It's harder to take this lesson because who is giving me the lesson? Myself? How do you teach yourself life lessons? Is this how? Am I learning how to live right now? Have I finally woken up?

> **Kevin:** Time is valuable. More so than anything. Some people, they are just going through the motions of life. Prisoners to the decisions of their past and the people they

surround themselves with. They are blind. Blind to the problem. Blind to the solution. Their vision works. It's a far worse problem. Blindness of the mind...What's the cure? Knowledge. It takes years of training yourself and pushing. Always make sure you are using your time efficiently and wisely. Question those around you. Power is a perception. Who is in control? Are you in control of yourself? Are you sure? Who keeps you in check? The age-old question. Who watches the watchers? Question everything, and don't spend time watching foolish watchers. That is a lesson that is invaluable. Some never learn it. Instead, they spend their time living under the direction of others...the blind minds...

He smiles. One last lesson.

> **Someone:** Why do I feel broken? You and Ashley. Normal people don't do this.

> **Kevin:** Everyone has their problems. Embrace the side of you that isn't normal. Who wants to be normal?

I nod. That is exactly what I needed to hear.

> **Kevin:** Give your dad what he needs…a friend…a son…

I nod again.

Kevin: And remember…the memory is real... you can come see me anytime…you will be okay…

The room gets foggy. I try to reach out and shake Kevin's hand, but the table keeps growing. He is further and further away. Foggier and foggier. Gone.

Winding Down

I don't go back to school. It is late in the year already and with my diagnosis, as well as Dad's issues, it just isn't the right time to be focused on academics. The school is going to let me challenge the finals off-site. As long as I pass them all, I will graduate still.

Dad is basically surgically attached to me for the next few months. We watch almost every movie we have ever watched again. I had forgotten how much I liked the original *Alien* and *Star Wars*. I also had forgotten how much I just liked spending time with him watching movies.

A few months pass. My counselling is helping me. I have to be strong for Dad. This is not the time for me to quit. I learn to use my circle to introduce people. I make sure to always talk about new people with my closest friends. Jogging and writing are important. They help me keep the stress down. I share my writing now. It's getting better. I still see Kevin occasionally, when I have those deep questions about life.

286

Around June, Dad and I were at the doctor's together. I can tell he isn't getting better. The chemo has sucked his vitality away. His hair is gone. He has lost lots of weight. We are sitting in front of the x-ray board. The doctor says this is a normal brain. He then brings up Dad's. It is littered with all these black patches. Some pretty big. Inoperable.

You would think that this would crush me, but I feel at peace with it. Happy that I gave Dad what he wanted the last few months. We did manage the paperwork to get out of the hospital for a couple of hours a few days later. We use the time to go see *Super 8*. One last movie.

Dad is haggard, but the idea of watching a movie in the theatre brings out a tiny spark. The smell of the popcorn. The taste of the fountain pop. The sticky floors. The giant screen. These are the memories of him I want. *Super 8* is a throwback to classic monster movies. It feels like Abrams made this movie specifically for Dad. A going-away present. Popcorn, soda and a big screen will never feel as good as they do today.

It isn't more than a week after that before I find myself sitting in his hospital room. My friends come. A few of Dad's coworkers. It is a long day. Uncles and cousins, most of which I barely know, cycle in and out. It is late in the evening. I pull up next to him real close.

Someone: Hi, Dad. You there?

No response.

Someone: Well. Here goes.

I grab his hand and squeeze. He squeezes back just a little. Still some fight.

>**Someone:** I'm sorry. I wish I had been there this last year. I wish I could pull all your cancer out. I wish my schizophrenia wasn't a problem. I wish I had answers...

I adjust in my seat, getting in closer.

>**Someone:** I won't let it run my life anymore. I am in control. I know who I am. I got this.

Tears are rolling down my face. He squeezes harder.

>**Someone:** Mark my words on this day. You will live forever inside me. Inside every accomplishment I ever do. My life has a purpose. A path.

I sit there holding his hand for another half-hour. Eventually, in the night, the slow beep of the machine fades into one solid beep. I don't leave his side until the doctors pull me away.

Eulogy

THERE are hundreds of people. Everyone is sitting, fixated on the podium. Most wear black. I recognize faces: Erica, Caleb, Geoffrey, Samantha. This is the moment when I get to honour Dad forever, if I can choke out the words. The room is quiet. The eyes are on me. I hunch down on the podium. Bury my head. Stay still. Just trying to gather myself.

> **Someone:** Life is complicated. Things go well. Things don't. You can't control everything. Some things are inevitable. No matter what you do, you can't go back in time. You can't change the past. What you can do is use the past to change the future.

A pause and scan of the room.

> **Someone:** You lose things. You lose things you did with people. You lose people. It hurts more than anything in the world. You feel like you could never go on. The world gets heavy, like a thousand wet blankets lay

on top of you. The air gets thick. You can't breathe.

Try to breathe. Take a breath. That's it. You are getting through this.

    Someone: Time passes.

A deep breath to gather myself. I shut my eyes. Let the people here feel what I feel. Let them into my mind. Come with me on a journey.

    Someone: Your wounds heal. You remember. The air gets lighter.

A really long pause. Let them get lost. I can see people starting to well up. I stay strong.

    Someone: Bad times. Good times. Some of the best feelings you ever had. Unforgettable.

Silence save for the people starting to lose their control and let out the tears.

    Someone: Learn to live with the loss. Use it as inspiration. Recreate the feelings you had with them so their essence lives on. Do you feel it? You must feel something? Let it flow. Get lost in that feeling.

Another long pause.

    Someone: What you just felt. It's special...and hard...and rare. It goes away as

fast as you find it. Then you chase it the rest
of your life.

I can see the dust sparkle as it catches the light
coming through the church window. It's magical.

> **Someone:** Everything I do, I do for you.
> Forever.

I understand what it means to lose someone you love.
I understand the pain Geoffrey has felt. How Caleb
and Samantha feel. It is all making sense. I put my
index finger and middle finger to my heart then raise
those fingers into the sky slowly, letting the emotion
go into the universe for everyone to feel. I walk off in
silence and just shut down. That was a hard place to
go.

Farewell

MY situation is most certainly unique. I am on the verge of adulthood and kind of homeless. Dad had his finances together. He left me some money in an education trust. I don't have to worry about a job or house at the moment. My uncle has graciously offered me a place to stay, but it isn't what I am looking for. I want to change. The doctors say I am ready to try the real world again. It has been months now. They are happy with my progress. My writing and jogging are good for balancing me back out. I also have a good system in place to make sure I am doing reality checks. Don't get lost on a path without touching base with my circle. It will be a process, but there is no reason I can't go to college eventually. I will have to live with this forever, but the memories of Dad fuel my desire to keep pushing forward.

I ace all my placement tests. Tests were never hard for me. Academics were the easy part of school. It was the social side that drove me bananas. English was a breeze; I had pushed myself and learned so much. It was night and day comparing me today to

292

me nine months ago. Business was even easier. I was so invested in the material, it just flowed from me.

My plan isn't fully developed, but I have my eyes set on being undeclared with on-site dorm living. I am going to try writing and business at the college level. I want to go to a college far away. Where no one knows who I am. A clean start. See if I can find my place. Do something for me. Listen to my heart. Become who I want to be. Become someone.

There is one last thing. Our swan song to high school and teenage life. The fruits of our labour for the year. Grad camping. My emotions are mixed. So much has happened in the last few months. I debate not going, but figure it will be a good opportunity to get my mind off Dad for a night. I don't know if I have the strength to face all the people I knew before. I am a different person now than I was a few months ago. My journey has aged me far beyond my years. It is hard to look at these people the same way. Most of them don't know what real loss is. They don't know what real problems look like. I have danced with the devil inside my mind and am still standing. They all seem soft.

I can't take the bus. It will be too hard. I will feel trapped. Instead, my uncle has agreed to drive me. He is a cool guy. Funny, it took Dad passing to get to know him. We drive for about two hours. I get there an hour late. We have a special group campsite away from the regular campground. My uncle is going to hang around with the other parents. He says if I feel like getting out, just call. He will come back in a second to get me. He is just trying to support me, but I honestly don't need it.

I have essentially become a legend. Fueled by rumours. Only some of them are true. I don't really care anymore either. The opinion of strangers is no longer something that influences my life. I am driven by the opinion of one man. The man who raised me. Do what he would want me to do. Make him proud. Everything else is just noise.

Everyone is being the nicest they have ever been to me. Offering up their stuff. Asking how I am feeling. What it was like. It is as if everyone is afraid I am fragile, when in actuality, I am now made of iron.

Most of the class has settled in. Some people have solo tents. Others are sharing. I brought nothing. I am happy to sleep outside if it comes to that. The cold night air feels great after spending months in a hospital. All you can do in the hospital is sleep, think, and write. Now that I am out, I want to do just about anything else.

A giant fire starts pretty soon after we get there. There is ample food. Enough hot dogs, s'mores, and salads to feed a small country. Everyone is letting loose. Even the parents are being cool. We are basically adults now. Mature adults that randomly break into song. *Friday* by Rebecca Black makes an appearance.

In talking, I find out Trevor had left the school. Once football season ended, he had no more skin in the game. He already had a scholarship. He didn't need the social stress that I had brought his way, and he definitely didn't care about finishing school. I am sure his college will just help him forge documents to ensure he can catch footballs for them in September. Sad thing is that guy will probably be rich and famous one day. The world is a funny place.

I find Amanda, the Locker Girl. She is roasting marshmallows. She doesn't talk my ear off. She has mellowed. Maybe it is me who has mellowed. It has been so long since that party where I jettisoned her.

> **Amanda:** How are you?

> **Someone:** A little confused, a little sad, a lot okay.

> **Amanda:** I can only imagine.

> **Someone:** The weirdest thing. The ticket to people's hearts is showing them just how crazy and messy you are.

She chuckles

> **Someone:** What?

> **Amanda:** Yes. It's true.

> **Someone:** I am trying to find words for you. It's hard.

> **Amanda:** I forgive you.

Someone: I was a bad person. I was mean. I didn't listen. I didn't let you in.

Amanda: It's okay.

Someone: My mind feels strange. Like a bomb went off, and it should have killed me...but it didn't. Now I am just trying to piece it all together and figure out what is next. Picking up the shrapnel of my life.

Amanda: Second chances are hard to find.

Someone: Sometimes you don't get them. Sometimes you will wish you had gotten a second chance. What would my life have been like had I been nice to you? My dad still would have died, but I would have reacted differently. I am just left to wonder if the last couple of months could have been different.

Amanda: Don't get too caught up in the what-ifs. I am always trying to overachieve. It's exhausting.

She stops...I actually look deeply into her eyes for the first time.

Someone: You are pretty cool.

We both nod. I need to go find my old friends now. It has been a while since we all have gotten together to just chill. I find my way to the familiar faces. After the meet-and-greet session, we sit down and just talk like old times.

> **Someone:** So are Caleb and Erica a thing?

They both chuckle and light up.

> **Caleb:** It was a thing a few months ago. Now it's more. Erica and I are both going to travel. Spend a good six months abroad. Then make our next decision.

> **Someone:** That's amazing. That's what you wanted. So cool.

I am happy for them. Big smile.

> **Someone:** This is hard to get out, but I am leaving too.

They don't look all that surprised though.

> **Someone:** I need a fresh start.

> **Erica:** You do. Where you off to?

> **Someone:** I honestly don't know. Going to go back to my old town, and then start a new life.

> **Caleb:** You heard about our buddy Geoffrey over here?

Caleb shoots a glance over his way.

Someone: No.

Caleb urges him.

Geoffrey: I am going to Juilliard.

Someone: That's so cool.

Geoffrey: Full scholarship.

Someone: Wow, man.

I think about it.

Someone: What about your mom?

Geoffrey: It's hard, but it's time. She would want me to live my life.

Caleb: So this is kind of goodbye?

We all stop and pause. Who knows where we will all be in a few months?

Someone: I have to say something. I didn't know what a real friend was. What real love was. Now I do. You saved me from myself. Taught me how to live and feel. Thanks so much for waking me up.

We all get in and hug again.

Geoffrey: You know, Caleb saved me too, right? It was years ago, and I was in a dark

298

place. He pulled me out. He saved Samantha too. She thinks none of us know anything but we all know her story, and we know it because Caleb was the one who intervened. He just keeps doing that. It's a talent.

Erica: Some people are just awesome. They give and give and give. It's hard to find them.

Someone: Hold onto that one.

I nudge Erica towards Caleb. She reaches into her pocket and hands me something. It is some of the Shaman's tools. I know one day I will go back, but it won't be soon. I will need to be ready. It will be years before I gain back confidence and trust with myself.

We spend the next hour being our normal, weird selves. I mainly get reflective about my imaginary friends. It is a pretty good story and we all know it. They fill me in on the last couple months. Eventually, Caleb leans in close to me.

Caleb: Samantha's been talking about you again.

Someone: Where is she?

Caleb: I don't know. She's been down. She's here somewhere. I think you would be good for her. Go find her.

I give him a hug. That hug is hard. He saved me, and now I am going to leave him because I feel I need the fresh start. I don't even fully understand why I am going; it just feels right, and I am going to trust my gut from now on. I reach over to Geoffrey and hand him a piece of paper. It is one of the things I did in the hospital. Two songs. One about lost love and the other about Dad. I can't sing though, so I hand it over to a person who can actually do something with it. He opens it and gives me a thumbs up. His grin tells me he is surprised.

The night sky is starting to light up with the stars. Samantha still eludes me. They have a giant telescope that Amanda had brought from the planetarium as well as an astronomer to help guide us through the sky. Amanda is a go-getter and did a good job with our grad. I take a quick peek. It is cool. The sky is so big, so much to learn if you want to. I like the unknown feeling. The wonderment of looking at something you don't understand.

The hopeless wanderer searching the campground. I have been wanting to see her badly, and now my schedule is clear. Where is her mind at?

She is alone. Sitting on a picnic table bench. Away from the group. Around the corner, behind some trees, and overlooking the lake. All the stars have come out now.

> **Someone:** What are you doing?

> **Samantha:** Thinking.

> **Someone:** Do you want to come to the star-gazing thing?

Samantha: Not really. I would rather be alone.

Someone: Oh, sorry.

Samantha: No. You can stay. I mean alone from the group. You don't count. You aren't like them.

I come and sit down next to her. She is looking up.

Someone: You been watching much anime?

Samantha: No.

Someone: What you been doing?

Samantha: Thinking.

Someone: About what?

Samantha: What's it like?

I return a puzzled look.

Samantha: What's it like to be diagnosed? To lose everything.

Someone: For a little bit, the weight of the world lifted away. It was the answer to every question I had been asking myself. The grand riddle solved, but now I have a new problem. I don't trust myself. I don't know what is real. Are you real? How can I know?

Samantha: What if I feel that way? I always feel like something is wrong and I can't put my finger on it. Can I get there? Can I get my answer?

I wonder. How did I get here? Can I provide a blueprint? Can I help others? Was my path even the right path? It was messy and dangerous. I can't answer that question right now. Minutes go by. I am just drawing blanks.

Samantha: Tell me some more about Ashley and Kevin.

I don't want to show her how weird I am at my core. Why does it matter? This is the last chance. Might as well show her everything I got.

Someone: Kevin was like the adult I wish I could be. He was everything I looked up to. His advice was perfect. He made me smile when I was down. His energy was infectious.

Samantha: Be like him.

Someone: He isn't real.

Samantha: So?

I think about it, but she is right. Be like Kevin...

Someone: Ashley was the friend I needed and then became a plague. The balance to Kevin. The negative energy. Indulgence.

302

B.A. Bellec

The run away from everything forever kind of person. It was weird trying to reconcile them both.

She looks into my eyes. I am vulnerable. She can see the confusion.

> **Samantha:** Sorry.
>
> **Someone:** About?
>
> **Samantha:** About your dad.
>
> **Someone:** That one stings the most. So much wasted time. I could have spent this last year with him.
>
> **Samantha:** You don't really have much. It's really sad.
>
> **Someone:** I had lots though, and now I have myself. Is that better? How do you put a value on finding yourself?

Now she can't answer. Minutes go by. We're just thinking.

> **Someone:** It's getting cold.
>
> **Samantha:** It's okay.
>
> **Someone:** Here.

I take my jacket off and give it to her. She puts it half-on and then invites me in close to share the other half.

Someone: Any regrets?

Samantha: About what?

Someone: About anything?

Samantha: Absolutely. I have regrets about lots of things in my life. At the same time, I know I have made some really good decisions to bad problems.

She pats herself on the stomach. I think about the car accident. How one event in life can have so much ripple. Would what happened to my mom happen to Samantha? Can I do anything?

Someone: Do you know what happened to my mom?

Samantha: No.

Someone: I do now.

Samantha: What?

Someone: I heard it in the hospital. She was in a car accident and lost her unborn child. I would have had a sibling. That is crazy to think about. It destroyed her. Bad choice, after bad choice for years after that. It's hard to deal with the pain but no letting go is worse. Trust me.

She doesn't answer but I see her processing. I think back to that letter I wrote.

>**Someone:** Why can't we try? Why can't you come with me on a journey? I want to take a huge trip. Wake up my soul.

>**Samantha:** We're not ready for a relationship. We have been so stupid. Just think about all the dumb things we have done this year.

>**Someone:** Let's be stupid together for a while.

>**Samantha:** I am done being stupid. I want a fresh start.

>**Someone:** I want a fresh start too. We can do it together.

>**Samantha:** I am alone for the first time in years and I am actually okay with it. Part of that is you. You showed me how to be alone.

I squeeze her a little harder with my arm. Letting her know I get it. Stargazing souls who met at the wrong times in their lives. We spend the rest of the night sharing the last of our secrets. It is lots of thinking. Cherished time together. Savouring the moment.

I know I will always wonder why I let her go…why didn't I fight harder? I was so close. It felt so real…but I did let her go. A night I will never forget. The closest I have ever been to someone spiritually.

There were many lessons the last year and I will certainly need a long time to put the puzzle together. One of the things that sticks to me the most. A bunch of weirdos who became lifelong friends, who help each other, who talk through the tough times. Life will pull us in a bunch of different directions. Family, love, education, career, health, relaxation. Find the balance. Know we will have a special bond forever. The weirdos who save each other. The weirdos who find each other in the dark.

The Missing Piece

MY car is packed with me, an iPad, and a moon lamp. That is all I need right now. The moon lamp to remember Dad. The car to answer my questions. The iPad to tell my story.

You might laugh at travelling with a moon lamp if you don't know my story, but that lamp means the world to me. It is a piece of Dad I can hold onto. When I look at that lamp, I remember all the movies. All the sacrifices he made for me.

I am checking in with the doctors, but that part comes in phases. As long as I keep up the checks, I don't get lost. My problems get worse if I leave them unchecked. That is true about everything though.

This town is so small. Coming back makes me chuckle. In a year, my growth has been exponential, and this place has stayed exactly the same. When I stop for gas, the attendant behind the counter is a familiar face. The liar from my dreams. She is yelling at a person on the phone and looks worn down. It seems like she really has her life together.

From there, I swing over to the school. I want to see
Dr. Drum, but don't really want to talk to her. I park
outside and wait. Just trying to remember everything
she told me. The doubt. The anger. The pain. Then I
think about Kevin. What it means. How can I
reconcile the fact that Kevin was nothing more than a
voice in my head? Ashley and all the bullying from
this place. Isolation, fear. It is lots to take in. I am
done worrying about old problems. Now I look for
solutions.

Eventually, she does leave. She slowly makes her
way from the school to her car. Her bones are old.
Her thinking is old. She stops for a cigarette at her car
door. Slowly poisoning herself. Everybody has their
vices though. Who am I to judge? What I don't like is
her telling others their path is wrong, but then
walking out the door and sucking on chemicals.
There is no point in trying to talk to her. She won't
accept that I have changed. She can't be reasoned
with. In her eyes, I will always be a useless parasite.
She is the one stuck. I am vibrating with energy.

After two hours of talking with the people around
town, I catch a break. It's a small town. Everyone
knows everyone. It is only a forty-five-minute drive.
Not that far. Kind of surprising. She was forty-five-
minutes away from every birthday or Christmas, yet
she never came once. Happy to leave this place
behind. This town feels like a cage. Thoughts bounce
around as I make the trek down the highway.

The building is falling apart. Some of the windows
are boarded up. Needles on the ground. It smells like
garbage. You don't have to buzz in. This is no home,

it is a prison for the lost and broken. I just walk right up to the door on the second floor. I knock. It opens as far as the chain lock will let it. I see most of her face. She snaps a few words out.

Old Woman: What do you want?

She is drained well beyond her years. Leather skin with sores on her face. Her hair is frizzled and grey. She has the vitality of Dad lying on his death bed. I spend a few seconds trying to process.

Someone: Oh, sorry, I think I have the wrong room.

Her clothes are tattered sweats. Nothing special.

Old Woman: I hate this place. Stop bugging me!

This is the first time I have seen my mother in so long I can't remember. I have photos where she is young and full of life. Those are the memories I will keep. I had to see what Dad had been hiding from me. I knew it wasn't going to be pretty. I'm glad I did it though, as it was the last thing on my checklist. Now it is time to move on.

It's a strange feeling being completely alone. No family. No job. No school. Just me and my troubled mind. How do I know which people are real? What makes something real? I don't have the answer today, but maybe one day I will.

Determination: The Finish Line

A N exhausted middle-aged man leans against the wall of the shower. Warm water runs down his back. His legs look like they are ready to buckle at any second. If it weren't for the wall, he would surely be on the ground. Off to the side in the shower sit his clothes. His number eighty-eight atop the pile. He hadn't bothered to take his socks off. The pain would have been too much. Instead, he just showers in them. The water turns them pink where there aren't holes revealing blisters and wounds.

The clock on the wall ticks, but the man barely moves. Eventually, he manages to shut off the shower and hobble over to a bench where he wraps himself in a towel and then just lies down. Each movement requires so much energy that just standing to open a locker is a task. He does it, pulling out a pair of black cargo shorts and a stylish red polo. Crippled by obvious pain, he slowly dresses.

A knock at the door. He groans. A beautiful woman enters and charges over to give him a big hug. She

radiates like a goddess. The hug almost topples the
man. Then she touches him on the shoulder. That's
their way of letting each other know, this is reality.
She is his lighthouse to keep his mind in check, and
that pinch is the beacon. He knows what it means and
he smiles.

Woman: Babe, I can't believe you did it!

Her smile is contagious.

Someone: We did it.

She embraces him again then helps him sit down after
realizing the embrace almost crippled him.

Woman: Let me wrap those feet.

She slowly removes the socks, his face clenched in
agony, to reveal feet that look like they might belong
to a burn victim or someone battling a flesh-eating
virus. Strangely, she doesn't seem put off. Just
another day wrapping up some bloody feet. With
great care, they apply gauze and get sandals on, then
they fix the man's hair into a bun. His polo leaves his
arm tattoo fully exposed: Not Done.

Woman: Do you want to shave?

Someone: No. I like it.

Woman: They want you in fifteen minutes
for a press conference.

He just lies down again on the bench. She leans over and gives him a giant kiss, then grabs a crutch and helps him to the door. The hallway is fairly short, maybe two hundred feet, a red curtain at the end. That red curtain looks like a black dot on the horizon.

Slowly, they hobble along. A crutch supporting one side, the woman, the other. As they approach, the buzz of a couple hundred people can be heard. When they finally break the curtain, a roar erupts. Clapping and cheering for a solid minute. The man slowly makes his way to a table where a woman is already sitting with a microphone in her hand.

> **Reporter:** You just won one of the premier ultra-marathons.

The crowd cheers again.

> **Reporter:** Two hundred and five miles over two and a half days. Over one hundred and fifty entrants.

The crowd cheers again. A quick scan reveals many of them look to be very fit and casual. It looks like a room full of runners.

> **Reporter:** Tell us, what are your first thought?

> **Someone:** It's hard to think; there is a lot of pain. It's really just kind of setting in right now in this room. Just coming back to reality.

312

Reporter: What got you through it?

Someone: My dad passed away when I was in high school. I dedicate every run to him. I wish he had been here watching, but I guess in a way he is always with me, helping me power through. There are some old friends too. Everyone has their battles. I even have my own internal battles.

He pauses for a second. Wipes his eyes.

Someone: My main motivation is my wife and our little girl.

He points over.

Someone: She is a rock, and without her, I would have nothing. She taught me how to feel alive again. How to accomplish amazing things. I was nothing. A clean slate. Then I met her, and she helped build me into a man. She guides me through life. I need her. I love that she came all this way just to wrap my feet when I can barely move.

The crowd chuckles.

Reporter: Were there any moments you thought about stopping?

Someone: One. I was halfway. No socks. No water. Hours from the next checkpoint. Off the trail. I really thought about it hard. Then I saw my tattoo: Not Done. A reminder. I am not done yet. Pick up your bloody socks and get moving again. I might have quit there ten years ago, but that day. Nope.

Reporter: Wow. Grinding deep. I see your feet are completely wrapped. Can we see the socks?

Someone: If someone wants to go back to the locker. I can't move. It would take me all day.

The crowd laughs again, and one of the assistants runs back. They are barely gone for a few seconds. The crowd gasps, and then small chatter between themselves takes over the room.

Reporter: What do we have?

Someone: Those are my socks from the last day and the shoes I ran the whole race in.

The shoes are falling apart. Tape holds them together. It was an on-the-run modification. Just wrap them in duct tape and get me back on the course. The socks. They aren't socks anymore. There are holes in them, and they are more pink than anything else. The room looks at them in amazement.

Reporter: How do you do that? How do you not think about shoes and socks like that? What did you think about out there? Where does that pain go?

Someone: You can't think about your feet. You'll stop. There was one thing that kept coming back. I started writing a book a long time ago. It kind of fell by the wayside. Life happened. Job, family, my struggles. For some reason, I just kept thinking about that half-finished dream. That year in my life. It's funny, you dream of running a huge race like this, and then while you are out there, you focus on a different dream. Maybe I will be able to use the next few recovery days to write the last few chapters of that book. Doubt I will be moving much.

Reporters: Any last words?

Someone: To anyone struggling with mental health, remember that you can get through this. Life is confusing and difficult. Find your support system. Jogging, writing, learning and a few important people. People are so important. My wife. My doctor. My therapist. People that will stand behind you and keep you pointed in the right direction. Design something that works for you. Get out. You can manage. You can always manage. There are days it will suck. Those days are just as important as the good days. You have to feel lows to feel highs. You have to feel confused to find clarity.

The crowd gives one last loud cheer with some extra vigour.

Reporter: There he is. Our champion.
Humble, but iron-willed.

He takes two fingers and puts them to his heart. Then
he raises them to the sky.

The End

B.A. Bellec

From The Author

W HAT is fiction and what is truth? Does it matter? Did I combine people from my life? Most certainly. Did I embellish certain aspects? Any good writer would. There is real loss in these words. It may not have been mine, but I felt it. Once you have felt deep pain, you will look back on your life and you will suddenly realize there were moments other people around you felt like this, but you didn't notice or help them because you had never felt it. You have to get hurt to find those people, and then you will wish you could turn back the clock. You can't. All you can do is give them a nod. Try to help them. Move forward to a better future.

To be honest, I didn't think I was going to publish a word of this. It all just presented itself in front of me as a coping mechanism. The story was there waiting, but I couldn't see it at first. It took me years of reflecting to find it and develop the skills. The hardest thing I have ever done, but the focus gives such a payoff.

Someone's Story

At some point in life, you will start asking questions the people around you can't answer. To continue your path of growth, you will have to turn somewhere else. You can expand your mind by going to university. You can enlarge your soul by pushing yourself in relationships. You will get to a point where you and no one you know has the answer. You can't explain the problem. You can't rationalize the decision. You see it, but you don't know how to proceed. You must take a leap of faith. You can never know for sure.

Meditation will teach you to accept. It will teach you to see paths you didn't see before. It will teach you how to dig deeper. Find pieces of you that didn't exist. Grow. Remove labels and change. Feel it all. The pain. The mistakes. The joy. The euphoria. You are reliving your worst day over and over until it doesn't mean anything. Release the pain. You are analyzing your biggest problems until they seem insignificant. You carry the weight of a friend. You carry the weight of a loved one. You carry the weight of a label. A problem. A project. The stresses of money, life, relationships, fear. They are holding you back. Life is hard. You are tired. Let go of those tired, hard thoughts.

Pure joy. Joy that defines you. If you look back over your life, which moments stand out? Listen to the world. Let it guide you to those moments. You might find yourself isolated. You might find yourself surrounded by strangers. Something beautiful will come of it, just keep listening. Not every decision will be perfect. Adjust your path. Keep moving forward. Your heart knows what it wants. Push. Dig. Find your voice. Keep growing.

Failure. Realize every failure was just you trying something new. To accept the fear of failure as a part of life. You will learn so much from your failures. They will drive your greatest accomplishments. One day, you will look back at all your failures. You will see joy. Joy you tried. Take a meeting and fail. Try to write and fail. Take a job and fail. Don't give up.

Fail.

Learn.

Adjust.

Grow.

I hope you learned something, and thank you for coming on a journey with me. If you liked what you read, please give me just a few more minutes:

- Find my website: babellec.com
- Follow me on Twitter: @b_bellec
- Leave a review on Amazon
- Leave a review on Goodreads
- My YouTube channel has original music inspired by this book

- Donate to the Canadian Mental Health Association

Then use this story as the inspiration to go follow your dreams.

I am not done. I put the finishing touches on this book and jumped right into my next project. *Pulse* is coming soon. It's a totally different beast!

B.A.